Ski Mask Cartel

T.J. Edwards

**Lock Down Publications and Ca$h
Presents
Ski Mask Cartel
A Novel by *T.J. Edwards***

Ski Mask Cartel
Lock Down Publications
P.O. Box 870494
Mesquite, Tx 75187

Lock Down Publications
Like our page on Facebook: Lock Down Publications @
www.facebook.com/lockdownpublications.ldp
Cover design and layout by: **Dynasty Cover Me**
Book interior design by: **Shawn Walker**
Edited by: **Lauren Burton**

T.J. Edwards
Stay Connected with Us!

Text **LOCKDOWN** to 22828 to stay up-to-date with new releases, sneak peaks, contests and more…

Thank you!

Ski Mask Cartel
Submission Guideline.

Submit the first three chapters of your completed manuscript to ldpsubmissions@gmail.com, subject line: Your book's title. The manuscript must be in a .doc file and sent as an attachment. Document should be in Times New Roman, double spaced and in size 12 font. Also, provide your synopsis and full contact information. If sending multiple submissions, they must each be in a separate email.

Have a story but no way to send it electronically? You can still submit to LDP/Ca$h Presents. Send in the first three chapters, written or typed, of your completed manuscript to:

LDP: Submissions Dept
Po Box 870494
Mesquite, Tx 75187

DO NOT send original manuscript. Must be a duplicate.

Provide your synopsis and a cover letter containing your full contact information.

Thanks for considering LDP and Ca$h Presents.

T.J. Edwards
Dedications

This book is dedicated to my amazingly, beautiful stomp down wife, Mrs. Jelissa Shante Edwards, who knows firsthand what this Ski Mask life is all about. I've had to feed our family many nights using that to make it happen. But, for you, I had to find another way because you deserve the best, and my place to be is beside you, protecting you at all times. You're my motivating force that keeps me going. No matter how old you get, you'll always be *my* baby girl. So, deal with it. I love you forever and always. Your husband.

Ski Mask Cartel
Acknowledgments

Shout out to Cash and Shawn. I love ya'll with all my heart... not only as a C.E.O and C.O.O, but as brother and sister. This is me and my wife's home. You already know that our loyalty is sealed in blood. Mad love to the entire LDP family.

Much love and respect to my hittas: Von Walker, Antoine Drew Jr aka Burleigh Wood, Paul "Trey-Six" Westmoreland and my big homie Edward Wilson aka "E". Free ma dudes man and release these animals back to the jungles they were stripped from.

T.J. Edwards

Chapter 1

"Racine! Racine! Wake up, please, baby! That nigga in there beatin' on my momma again. Please go in there and help her before he try and kill her like he did last week!" Kenosha hollered, trying her best to get me out of the bed.

I sat up and shook my head. It seemed like every time I spent a night over at my baby momma's house it was always some bullshit jumping off between her parents, and that was why most times I came over I made sure Kenosha had her and my daughter, Madison, ready to go and waiting for me on the porch.

I ran my hands across my face and took a deep breath. Looking at the clock, it was three in the morning, and I had just got there about an hour ago, put my daughter in my arms, and fell asleep with her lying on my chest.

Madison was five years old and the love of my life. Me and her mother brought her into the world when we were both just 16 years old and had been trying to figure things out ever since then.

A plate crashed somewhere off in the distance, followed by a loud-ass boom. It sounded like something had fallen over. Then I heard muffled voices. I guessed it was her parents doing their usual thing, and I just didn't feel like getting in the middle of that shit.

Kenosha got up and opened the door, making it so we could hear everything loud and clear. As soon as she did, another plate shattered loudly, and the sound caused my daughter, Madison, to wake up crying.

Now, I was pissed off.

She sat up in bed and pulled the covers off herself before crawling across it and wrapping her slim arms around my neck. "Daddy, I'm scared. I don't want John to hit my grandma no more. I don't want him to kill her like my momma say he is."

She hugged me tighter and I could hear her sniffling under me. Her body trembled, and I could tell she was really scared. I wrapped my arms around her and kissed her on the forehead. "Baby, don't worry. I'm not gon' let nothin' happen to yo' grandma. I promise, okay?" I said, holding her a little tighter. I didn't like nobody scaring my daughter. Madison was my heart, and there was nothing or nobody in the world I loved half as much as her.

Kenosha thought about stepping out of the bedroom when Janet appeared with a can of beer in her hand. She looked drunk and smelled horrible. I looked her over from head to toe in disgust because I remembered how she had looked when I'd first met Kenosha, back then she was fine as hell, but that was before the crack had taken over her world.

"There you go, baby," Janet said, trying to catch her breath. She was a caramel-skinned female with short hair cut into a style that was in need of a touch-up. She wore a white t-shirt that was way too big for her, and it was dirty as if she was using it for a cleaning rag or something. I couldn't see what she had on underneath it because the shirt hung so low, but I figured she was wearing some kind of biker shorts, which would have been her usual attire.

She swallowed, then reached out and touched Kenosha's shoulder. "Baby, you said you put $500 in my purse last night to go toward the rent, am I correct?" she asked before taking a long swallow from the can of St. Ides.

Kenosha frowned. "Momma, why you askin' me this? You already know that's what I gave you. I counted it out in front of yo' face and told you that you needed to add it with the $600 you got because the

Ski Mask Cartel

landlord been hittin' my phone for the last week askin' about his rent. He threatenin' to evict all of us."

This was news to me and something Kenosha hadn't mentioned. I had given her that $500 earlier in the day, but she didn't tell me what exactly she needed it for, and due to the fact she was my daughter's mother, I didn't feel like she was obligated too. I felt like my job was to make sure whenever she needed anything, I was able to provide it for her.

Janet nodded her head and took another deep breath. "Well, this nigga swearing up and down all of the money in my purse is his. He think he finna go smoke my shit up, and I ain't having that. So, I need you to tell him that $500 was yours."

Kenosha frowned. "Dang, I hate always getting in the middle of y'all drama. Y'all do this every other day. This stuff getting old, momma, fo' real." She looked at the floor as if she were in deep thought.

Kenosha was around five-foot, four inches tall and about 120 pounds with naturally curly hair and Hershey brown skin. She had a prominent mole on the right side of her upper lip that I loved. Even though we had a daughter together, me and her weren't necessarily to-gether, though I held a deep respect for her on all levels.

She stepped into the hallway. "Where's John at right now, momma?" She sounded as if she were defeated.

John must have not been that far away, because it seemed like as soon as she stepped out of the room he stepped into Janet's face and bumped his forehead against hers. "Bitch, I said that's my muthafuckin' money, and I'm gon' spend it however I choose to. And I don't give a fuck what this bitch say, or nobody else, for that matter." He pointed his finger at Kenosha, and she took a step back.

11

T.J. Edwards

"Get you damn finger out of my face, John. I done already told you about that. I'm getting tired of you disrespecting me in front of my daughter."

Though she was talking to him, she refused to look him in the eye, as if she were afraid of him. That made me feel some type of way. I could feel Madison shaking in my arms. She was shaking as if it was freezing cold in the room.

"Momma, please don't make him mad. I don't want him to whoop you like he do me when you at work. Please, momma," she whimpered.

It felt like the entire world stopped after I heard her say what she said. I got to imagining this nigga putting his hands on my daughter in any way, and I felt my head getting hot.

Before I could even ask her what she meant about him whooping her, Kenosha snapped, "Nigga you put yo' hands on my baby again? I told you that you not her muthafucking grandfather. You ain't got no right putting yo' hands on my child!" she hollered with her eyes closed.

John grabbed Janet by the throat and slammed her up against the wall with authority, making the back of her head bounce off it. "Bitch, you gon' let this ho talk to me like that? Huh? This bitch stay wit' us, and this how you let her get down on me?" He frowned, and from his face I could tell he was choking her with a lot of his might.

Janet squirmed against him, trying to pry his hands loose by pulling at his fingers with her own. "Ack! Ack! Let me. Ack!"

Kenosha had seen enough. She stepped forward and slammed her fists downward against his hold trying to break them apart. "Let my momma go! I'm tired of you putting yo' hands on her. This shit is getting old. You need to–"

12

Whap! He backhanded her so fast, catching me off guard.

I had been sitting on the bed holding my daughter, trying to get her to calm down because she was shaking so bad it was spooking me. I had never felt her do that before. I didn't find out until later he had been abusing my daughter physically by whooping her on a regular basis. But after I saw him backhand Kenosha and heard her yelp as if he really hurt her, I picked my daughter up and carried her to the closet in the room, opened the door, and put her down inside of it before kneeling.

"Baby, I need you to close this closet door, and don't come out of here until I come and get you. Do not worry. I am not going to leave without you, I promise. Do you understand me?" I asked, hearing a bunch of tussling outside of the room door.

She nodded. "Please don't leave me, daddy. I'm scared of John. He hurt my mommy, too." Tears fell down her cheeks and she continued to shake.

More tussling and rumbling ensued behind me. I knelt on one knee and kissed her on the forehead. "I promise, baby. Just let me go handle this." I closed the door and turned around with a serious mug on my face. I jogged out of the room, and by the time I got into the living room, John was straddling Janet, choking the life out of her with sweat pouring down the side of his face.

"I told you, bitch. I told you about playing wit' me. That's my money. All of it. Every muthafucking penny." He squeezed harder.

Kenosha was balled into a corner of the living room with blood running from the corners of her mouth, tears streaming down her cheeks, shaking like Madison.

I turned to John, looking down on him before cocking back and swinging forward, connecting with his jaw so hard he flew sideways off Janet. As soon as he fell off her, she took in a big gasp of air and put both of her hands to her throat, probably thankful she was able to breathe again. She lay on her back with her eyes wide open and her tongue out, coughing.

John jumped to his feet. "Nigga, what the fuck you putting yo' hands on me fo'? What, you trying to save these bitches?" He held up his guards, acting like he was ready to fight.

I didn't give a fuck about none of that. All I kept imagining was this nigga hitting my daughter and causing my baby mother to bleed. I already had it in my mind that I was getting ready to fuck this shit up. I rushed him as he swung a haymaker and busted my eye. I saw blue lightning, but it didn't stop me from catching him with a three-hit combo: one to his jaw, a left hook to his mouth, then I grabbed his head and jumped into the air, slamming my knee into his face and causing blood to squirt out of his nose. "Bitch-ass nigga."

He started to fall backward, and I rushed him again, tackling him into the wall in the living room. The walls were basically cheap plaster. That's how most of the apartments in Chicago were built. White smoke wafted into the air from the drywall. I heard my daughter scream off in the distance, but I was in a zone.

John groaned. "Aw. Aw. Come on, Racine, man. I can't breathe. I can't breathe. I need my asthma pump," he said, trying to make his way out of the hole in the wall. He started to wheeze loudly.

Behind us I could see Kenosha crawl over to Janet, wrapping her arms around her. Janet continued to rub her neck before accepting her daughter's affections. They both cried before Madison ran out of the room and into Kenosha's arms.

"Daddy! I want you!" she cried loudly, still shaking.

John continued to wheeze loudly. His chest rose and fell. He struggled to get out of the wall his body had fallen through. I looked to my right at the crying women and my daughter, and I couldn't help feeling more and more angry. I felt like John had in one way or another found a way to abuse each one of them. Once again, in my mind's eye, I imagined him putting his hands on my daughter and her breaking down from the pain he caused her, and I snapped. I waited for him to nearly work himself free of the big hole, before I rushed him at full speed, kicking him right in the chest with all my might. He flew backward into the wall loudly. *Whoom!* More of the drywall fell onto the carpet. He was now back in the room my daughter had previously been in. I looked through the hole and saw he was on his back, jerking his chest upward, wheezing loudly. One hand was in the air curled up, reaching for the unknown as he wheezed and struggled to breathe.

I stepped through it and stood over him, looking down on this bully of a man. There was no need for words. Every time he wheezed, it was like food to my soul. I had visions of blowing his brains out just to see his blood splatter across the carpet, but I had to factor in my daughter. She would already be traumatized enough.

Janet must have put two and two together of what was going on because she hopped to her feet. "Racine, he dying. He need his asthma pump or he gon' die! Wait a minute." She ran toward the back of the house.

I was taken aback. I couldn't believe she was still considering helping this nigga after everything he had done. So, I waited until she was outta sight, raised my Timms, and brought them down full speed right in the center of his chest, stomping the shit out of him. I tried to break every rib that protected his heart.

He sat up only to fall back downward, shaking like a fish out of water. White foam bubbled around his lips, his head backward, and his eyes were wide open and the color of red.

I heard her off somewhere throwing stuff around, looking for his pump. "I'm coming, John. I'm trying to find it, baby. I know you didn't mean to do what you did," she hollered with her voice cracking.

I was on my knees, choking this nigga like I had watched him do her. I wanted his bitch-ass to die every time I imagined him putting his filthy hands my daughter, or my baby mother. I wanted this nigga's lights out. I squeezed harder while he shook under me and tried to remove my hands weakly.

"Nigga, you finna die. I'll be damned if I let you put yo' hands on my people and you keep yo' life. Die, fuck-nigga, so I won't have to kill you later!"

As soon as I said the last part, the nigga started to shake real bad, and then all of the sudden the shaking got weaker, yet I held my grip tighter until he stopped altogether. Only then did I stand up and look down on him.

Janet ran into the room and dropped to her knees in a panic, so I took a step back. She rubbed John's chest, took the asthma pump, and put it to his lips so the mist went into his mouth. But it was pointless. He was already dead. She sprayed the mist again and again before her eyes got bucked. She laid her head on his chest, as is she were listening for a heartbeat. After seeing there was none, she started to panic. "No, no, no. Please, God, no. Don't let my man be dead. I need him. Please, Father."

She took the pump, put it to his lips, and squeezed it repeatedly before Kenosha came into the room and pulled her off him.

"Momma, get up. That nigga dead. We gotta get him out of here or we all going to jail," she said, pulling her by the back of her shirt.

Madison ran over and hugged both of my legs. She looked terrified. I was hoping her seeing the nigga's

Ski Mask Cartel

dead body wasn't gon' screw her up for the long term. I just wanted to protect my baby.

"Daddy, I'm scared, and I wanna leave wit' you," she whined.

Janet continued to cry and moan over John, and I was ready to get rid of this nigga and move on. I pulled Kenosha by her arm. "Look, take yo' mother and my baby girl, and y'all get up out of here. I'll handle this nigga."

"Why? Why did he have to die, though? I tried my best to find his pump. I really, really did. Y'all saw me. Oh, Lord, why did you take my man away from me? I need him," Janet cried.

After Kenosha took our daughter out to my car, she came back, and it took us twenty minutes to get her mother out of the house. She kept on crying and swearing up and down she didn't mean for him to die. I personally couldn't understand how a woman could take so much abuse from a man and still feel so much pain after God finally took him out of her life.

I didn't have much time to dwell on what she was feeling. I knew I had to get rid of this nigga's body, and as crazy as it may seem, I was looking forward to it.

T.J. Edwards

Chapter 2

Two hours later, my cousin Tez finally showed up with his tool kit. My cousin was my right-hand man and had been ever since we were five years old. We were both the same age, 23, and had the same birthday. He was born an hour before me, and he made sure he always reminded me of that every chance he got.

Tez was born and raised in Chicago just like me, and the summer before we had lost five of our closest homies to the streets. If I was to say my temper was horrible, then I didn't have an adjective for Tez's. That nigga ain't have no sense. I mean none whatsoever. My cousin loved that beef shit and was a super gangbanger.

I turned on the cold water in the tub and laid John on his side as my cousin handed me a big-ass ridged knife. "Man, where the fuck you be getting all of this shit, nigga?" I asked, looking him over closely.

He knelt on the tub on the side of me and tossed his long dreads over his shoulder before taking the knife out of my hand. "Jo, let me see this muthafucka 'cuz I been waiting to body this nigga anyway."

I stood up and looked down on him as he took the knife and slammed it into the bottom of John's fat stomach, right around his waistline, before pulling the knife upward, then down again. He then handed me the knife, took four fingers on each hand, and ripped open the slit in John's belly.

All at once his blood rushed out of him as if it were a bucket of red water. It pooled around his naked body before slowly going down the drain.

Tez pulled him open even more, grabbing the knife from me to cut more of his skin that was in the way. "I got some crazy connects that love hunting deer and shit. The same tools they be using to slice open them animals is the same ones I be using on these fuck-niggas. I love this shit." He smiled his dark-skinned face and went back to work on John. "After we drain this nigga, we gon' take him down stairs and chop him up. I wanna save some this meat for my pits, too. They love this human flesh. I'm trying to get them to the point where I can release them on a nigga's ass and they'll eat him alive. I'm talking fucking a nigga up so bad all they leave behind is bones, and then they bury them muthafuckas on they own. My li'l niggaz already savages, but I got a li'l more training to do before they get on that level," he said before slicing a huge gash into John's throat.

The gash looked like a wide-open mouth that threw up blood. It leaked out of his neck and pooled into the drain before disappearing. This wasn't the first time I had watched my cousin go through this routine wit' a nigga, but it was the first time he'd done it at my baby mother's house. I always tried my best to watch him closely because I knew I needed to learn how to dispose of a nigga on my own. I pretty much had it down pat, but I was still just a little unsure of myself.

After we drained John of as much of his blood as we could, we wrapped him in three blankets and took him down into the basement. Tez pulled the cord on his chainsaw and started the blade. I hated the sound of that muthafucka because it always gave me a headache, that and the fact every order he gave me while he used it he had to holler at the top of his lungs. We were lucky Janet was the only tenant in the duplex at the time, because had there been another family that lived upstairs over us, we would have had to make other arrangements.

I picked up John's hairy-ass leg and pulled on it with my hands wrapped around his ankle. Tez pulled his mask down and straightened the goggles on his face before squeezing the trigger on the chainsaw to rev the blade even more, then he walked over and began to cut off John's limbs one at a time.

After we cut off all his limbs, we put them in a garbage bag and loaded them into the back of Tez's Mustang, then we drove down to the Chicago River and dropped his severed parts in piece-by-piece. Tez kept a portion of one of his thighs, saying he was gon' feed it to his pit bulls. I don't know if he did it or not, but it sounded like some shit he'd do.

Later that night at a little after ten, I found myself at one of the backyard craps games, strapped and ready to bust a move wit' my cousin. I had about $300 to my name, and we both needed to get our weight up. I don't know how much Tez had in his pocket, but due to the fact I had a daughter to support, I always tried to make sure I kept no less than a thousand dollars in my pocket at all times. I wanted to make sure if ever she needed anything, I would be in a position to make sure she got it, and that went for Kenosha as well. I felt like it was my job to make sure she and my daughter were well taken care of at all times.

I slightly adjusted the .38 special in my waistband as I dropped down to one knee and watched the niggas around me real closely. It was early September and still kinda hot outside, so much so I was rocking Tom Ford shorts and an all-black t-shirt that hung low, so I could conceal my burner. I completed my ensemble with the black and white #9 Jordans. Most of the niggas around me at that time were in shorts and tees as well. I didn't know any of the niggas, but Tez said he did, and that was enough for me. All I cared about was damn near all of them had necks and wrists full of jewelry. I was already adding up their worth in my head.

Me and Tez were from the south side of Chicago, yet we were currently out west in the Holy City. The area was nicknamed the Holy City because it was infested with crazy Black Lords that were more often than not doped up on heroin and looking for a nigga to kill. I know that would have spooked most niggas from doing what we were about to, but me and Tez lived on the edge. It was all about the paper for us, no matter how dangerous the moves were.

Tez shook the dice in his right hand and looked around the circle at the men. "Muthafuckas might as well push that pile over here, 'cuz I'm on you niggas' asses!" he hollered and threw the dice. They rolled and came up on snake eyes, causing him to crap out. He shook his head. "Fuck!" He stood up for a minute, then knelt back down before looking up at me. "Jo, let me hold a fifty real quick so I can rape these niggas."

I stood up and looked down on him like he was crazy as he grabbed the dice, shaking them in his hand. The other men were smoking their blunts and sipping from pink Sprites. One older nigga in general with some long-ass gray and black dreads frowned his face and flashed a mouth full of diamonds of all colors. He curled his upper lip and mugged me. I wanted to say something to him right away, but I knew I had to stick to the script. So, I gave my cousin a crazy look before curling my upper lip.

"You crazy as a muthafucka, nigga. They raping yo' ass. You ain't about to get my money took. You cold right now. Know when to walk away."

Tez stood up and sucked his teeth loudly. "What? Nigga, if you don't give me that weak-ass fifty. I'll hit you when we get back to the trap, so it ain't like you giving me shit. You just letting me hold fifty until I get back to my money. Stop playin', nigga."

The older nigga wit' the diamonds in his mouth spoke up. "Say, Lord, why don't you let li'l bruh hold that fifty, so we can keep the gamble goin'? He feel like

he gon' bounce back, so let him do his thang." He
looked me up and down and flared his nostrils.

Yeah, I knew I ain't like that nigga right away. The
way he was looking at me and acting all cocky and shit,
telling me what to do wit' my money, it was all irritating
me. But once again I just stuck to the script. I pulled out
a hundred-dollar bill and gave it to him. "Look, nigga,
when we get back to the Trap, you better give my shit
back, 'cuz I ain't out here hustling for you just so you
can lose my paper to these niggas." I turned my back on
him and acted like I was finna get on my phone, walking
off a short way toward the alley.

I heard Tez say, "Yeah, whatever, nigga. I'm about
to rape these studs. Bets in, nigga. I bet 50, and I bet I
hit my point unseen for another 50."

As soon as he said he bet fifty and he'd hit point unseen for fifty, that let me know it was time to handle
bitness. I turned around in time to see him throw the dice
way out of the five-man circle. They rolled almost by
the back door to the house we were gambling behind.
All the men turned their heads to see what they read, and
that's when I jogged up to the older nigga with long
dreads and a diamond mouth and slapped him so hard
with my pistol I felt my wrist pop.

"Break yo' self, niggaz. Y'all already know what
this is," I said, watching blood drip out of the older
nigga's mouth.

He tried to go under his shirt to reach for his pistol
when Tez upped his .45 and smacked him across the jaw
wit' it. *Wham*! This time he fell to his stomach and
started to spit out his grill, one diamond tooth at a time,
before coughing up blood.

Two of the other niggas who were in the circle got
up and looked like they wanted to run. Tez grabbed one
by the neck and slammed the handle of his gun into his
forehead, knocking him to his knees and putting the

pistol to his forehead while it dripped his blood. "Bitch-ass nigga, lay it down and take all of that shit off right now," he said. "Strip naked, all of you niggas."

The other dude who had previously looked like he wanted to run was now lying on his stomach, taking his shirt off as best as he could. He had three thick gold herringbones around his neck with a gold chain and a yellow and black diamond five-point star that was lit.

I went into my drawers and flipped out the pillowcase, dumping all their contents inside of it. I took watches, chains, earrings, money, dope, anything and everything. I even took the niggas' clothes and pistols. Tez went from one nigga to the next, stripping them out of their shit violently. I mean yanking they shit straight off them.

The older nigga wit' dreads was the only one who had not stripped out of his clothes. I walked over to him, grabbed him by the dreads, and stuffed my .38 into his nose. "Bitch nigga, what's taking you so long? What, you can't follow directions or somethin'?"

He frowned and spit blood out of his mouth. Some dripped from his chin. I could see his teeth were jagged and most of them were missing now. "Nigga, you don't know who you fuckin' wit'. I'd advise you to rob these niggas and leave me the fuck alone, and maybe you'll be able to keep yo' life when I catch you, but right now it ain't looking so good."

I bucked my eyes as wide as they could go, looking down on this nigga like he had lost his mind. I gripped his dreads more tightly. "You think this shit a game, huh? You think I'm playing with you or something?"

He jerked his head away from me, then before I could even slam my pistol into his grill again, he tackled me and wound up on top of me, head-butting me straight in the face. I got dizzy right seeing two of him. He cocked his head back, ready to do it again, when I heard gunshots. *Boom! Boom! Boom! Boom! Boom!*

His blood splashed across my face before he fell on top of me, shaking. I pushed him off me and stood up on wobbly knees, my vision a little hazy. I saw Tez standing over him with a smoking .45, his face curled into a snarl.

Two of the naked niggas jumped up and took off running. One hit the fence in the backyard and got to running like his life depended on it. I ain't even have the strength to chase him. Tez aimed and busted at him three times, but it didn't stop him from getting away. I doubt if he even hit him. The other nigga ran through the gangway to the front of the house, where he got to whistling loudly.

Being from Chicago, I knew every hood had their own call to arms, and commonsense told me that was theirs. There was one other nigga lying on the ground naked with his hands above his head. He looked like he couldn't have been older than fifteen.

Tez skipped over to him and aimed the pistol at the back of his head. "Rest in peace, nigga."

The boy turned over to face him. "Please don't kill me, Lord. I don't wanna die. Please, man."

I didn't really see no reason to kill the li'l young dude. I felt like he was just out at the wrong place at the wrong time. Even though I knew the rules of the game told me I had to make sure he lost his life because he was a potential witness, it was just somethin' on my conscience that didn't want Tez to do it.

"Tez, fuck that li'l nigga. Let's go. You hear them calls?" I asked as more and more whistling sounded.

He mugged the shit out of the boy and shrugged his shoulders. "Fuck them niggas, cuz. I ain't letting this li'l nigga live. You know how the game go." He planted the

T.J. Edwards

barrel of his gun to the boy's forehead and pulled the trigger. *Boom! Boom!*

I saw the kid's head jerk twice, along with his brains splashing across the concrete.

Boom! Boom! Boom! Boom! Boom!

"Lord, there them niggas go. Chop they ass!" somebody said from a distance.

I didn't know where the shots were coming from, but I felt like I was about to get hit, so I ducked to the ground right alongside the dead older nigga.

Boom! Boom! Boom! Boom! Boom!

Bullets slammed into the garage, knocking wood from it. Tez ducked down and busted twice left, and then two more times to his right. "Let's get the fuck out of here!" he hollered and picked up the pillowcase with all their shit in it.

I followed him back into the alley, where we saw ten niggas running in our direction with pistols in their hands. As soon as I saw them, I stopped and busted. *Boom! Boom!*

They clapped back immediately with something that sounded fully automatic. *Pop-pop-pop-pop-pop-pop-pop! Pop-pop-pop-pop-pop!*

The alley lit up in the dark night. All the street lights had already been shot out, so it was the only light we were able to see, and it made me run my ass off.

Boom! Boom! Boom! Tez busted and followed me as I ran into somebody's backyard to run alongside their gangway only to come out onto another block full of niggaz who looked like they were trying to locate where the shots were coming from.

I didn't waste no time busting at they asses because I already knew had they been given the chance to clap at us first, they would have.

Ski Mask Cartel

Boom! Boom! Click! Click! Click! Fuck, I was out of bullets. Seeing as Tez wasn't busting, I imagined he was, too, so we really took off running.

I hopped another fence and my shirt got caught on the top of it and nearly made me shit on myself because I could hear plenty of footsteps behind us and heavy breathing.

"Where they go, Lord?" somebody said who couldn't have been more than twenty yards away.

I struggled to get my shirt untangled. Finally, I just took it off altogether and sprinted behind Tez, who was hauling ass. He hopped another fence and we came out onto a block where there was a man and a woman in the middle of the street arguing while they stood in front of a car that had both doors open.

It was like me and Tez saw it at the same time because before I could even make my way over to it, he was already headed in that direction.

I don't know what possessed him to park our stolen car five blocks over from the gamble we were supposed to rob, but I was regretting not saying nothing about it at that time. I also didn't know at the time how far away the gamble spot was going to be, but I wished I had paid more attention because I would have advised against the distance.

The man smacked the shit out of a short, heavyset woman. She fell to the ground and looked up at him, holding her face.

"Bitch, I'm sick of yo' mouth. Every time I say something to you, you gotta back talk. Now shut the fuck up and respect this pimping or I'm gon' kill yo' ass," he growled, looking down on her.

The headlights of the Cadillac illuminated the entire street. Once again, all the regular streetlights had been busted out, so the block would have been in utter darkness had it not been for the car.

T.J. Edwards

Tez ran up on the man before he could even see him and smacked him across the side of the head with the handle of his .45 before pushing him with all his might. The man flew and wound up on the ground right next to the woman, who struggled to get up.

Pop-pop-pop-pop-pop-pop! Bullets slammed against the back of the car, causing sparks to fly.

I ducked down behind a parked car as Tez jumped into the driver's seat of the man's Cadillac and threw open the passenger door. "Come on, cuz, them bitch-niggas gaining on you."

My heart was beating so hard in my chest it was making it hard for me to breathe. I was running out of breath and praying I didn't get hit by one of them bullets.

Pop-pop-pop-pop-pop! "Lord, kill them niggas! Hit they asses!" somebody yelled from a distance. The female on the ground screamed at the top of her lungs.

Pop-pop-pop-pop-pop-pop! More sparks flew across the back of the car. I waited until there was a pause in the fire and made a run for the open passenger door just as the back window shattered and Tez stepped on the gas, screeching down the block.

"Let's go, cuz! These niggaz in the Holy City crazy. I hate them Lord niggaz."

Pop-pop-pop-pop-pop! Boom! Boom! Boom! Pop-pop-pop-pop-pop!

Our car rocked from side to side. My passenger window shattered, and the glass landed in my lap. I ducked down, as more gunfire erupted, all aimed at our whip.

I don't know how we made it off that block and out of that hood, but by the grace of God we did. When it was all said and done, we made it away with a total of fifteen thousand dollars, eight pieces of jewelry, and four ounces of heroin. It wasn't much for what we had to go through, but all in all I had left with more than what I came with.

Chapter 3

Me and Tez plugged into the Ski Mask Cartel three weeks later after his baby mother's older cousin, Rayjon, flew in from New Jersey with large sums of money on his mind. Rayjon was a tall, skinny nigga with a short temper and a real handsome face that fooled most people. I heard he'd watched both of his parents get killed in cold blood by his own cousin. His father was supposed to have been some legendary nigga from back east by the name of Greed. And as the story was told to me, he had been the original leader of the Ski Mask Cartel before he was murdered by his nephew. I didn't know what was true or what was false. What I did know was Rayjon had plans on getting us rich, so he had my ear. And if Tez pledged his loyalty to him, then I would as well.

The first time I met Rayjon was on the south side of Chicago right after this little eight-year-old girl's funeral who had been killed by a stray bullet. I didn't know her like that, but I had seen her around in the hood and had a heavy heart for her family, so I wound up giving her mother five gees just, so she could give her daughter a proper funeral. I asked my cousin Tez to throw in another five so the family could have a little breathing room and he just wasn't wit' it.

"Racine, what the fuck I look like? That li'l girl's death ain't have shit to do wit' us, so why should we give her people anything?" He mugged the shit out of me and looked me up and down.

I shook my head and put my arm around the little girl's mother, walking off with her. I didn't feel like she should have had to listen to what he was talking about. I imagined if something had happened to Madison and Kenosha needed help and I wasn't around or something.

T.J. Edwards

I would hope somebody would do for her what I was for the little girl's mother.

Her name was Jill. She was kinda heavyset and had a real pretty face, though she looked severely depressed. I wrapped her into my arms and hugged her. "Say ma', don't listen to what my cousin talking about. He just being him. I want you to take this five stacks and put it toward whatever you need to. I know it's hard for you right now, so if you need a shoulder to lean on or anything else, you just let me know." Then I gave her my cell number.

She took the cash and my number before hugging me tight, sobbin' in my ear, and that shit made me feel horrible. I don't know why, but it just did.

While I was holding her, it started to drizzle outside, and Rayjon pulled up in a black-on-black Yukon Denali truck subbing something from Jay-Z.

Tez's baby mother, Raven, stepped out of the truck first, rocking a raw-ass Burberry skirt fit that had her looking colder than I ever saw her before. I found it strange she was jumping out of another nigga's whip right in front of Tez, and I just knew he was finna act a fool because he whooped her ass daily over every little thing. She was a short, high-yellow something with a banging-ass body and a jazzy attitude that kept her in trouble wit' him. So, it blew my mind when Tez walked up to Rayjon as he was getting out of the truck and they gave each other half of a hug. Tez turned around and waved me over. "Bro, leave that broad alone and come meet the homie. This that nigga right here. Trust me."

I gave Jill one final hug. "Remember what I said, li'l momma. If ever you need anything, hit me up, and I got you." I watched her nod and walk off as the rain stopped and the sun came back out full-bore.

When I got over to Rayjon, he sized me up quick before giving me a half hug. "What it does, kid? So, you the one my man's been telling me about. You get down wit' them hammers, right?"

I nodded and curled my upper lip. "Every day, all day, as long as them numbers right."

He laughed. "Well, fucking wit' me, them numbers gon' always be right. I told my li'l homie I'm gon' get you niggaz rich, and I meant that. My word is always bond. But you gon' find that out on yo' own. I just touched down, so let me get myself together and then I'm gon' invite you niggaz over so we can have a sit-down. Before the sunrise on Friday, I'ma make it so both of y'all got at least fifty gees in yo' pocket. Sound good?"

To me it most definitely did. I didn't know what he had up his sleeve, but for fifty gees I was all for it.

That night, as I was eating me a big bowl of cereal and watching *Everybody Hates Chris* wit' my daughter, Kenosha came into the room wit' tears in her eyes. Before my daughter could see it, I got up out of the bed and kissed Madison on her forehead. "Baby, I'll be back. Daddy gotta go talk to Mommy in the other room for a minute."

Madison frowned and crawled across the bed before she stood up in the middle of it. "Daddy, but I'm scared when you not wit' me. I don't want John to get me no more because he mad at me. Can't I just come wit' you?"

Every time I saw the fear written across her face, I was glad I killed that nigga John. Anybody who had my baby girl lookin' as scared as she was deserved to die, in my opinion, and if it was up to me I would have killed him repeatedly with a big-ass smile on my face. I grabbed her and wrapped her into my embrace. I could feel her little body against me, and it made me melt. I loved my daughter, and it was my job to protect her at all costs.

T.J. Edwards

"Baby, we're just gonna be right outside of the door, so don't worry because Daddy isn't going anywhere. I got you, and I will never let anybody hurt you ever again. You're my baby girl. Do you understand me?" I said, making sure my voice was soothing and comforting.

She picked up her teddy bear from the bed and lowered her head. "Okay, Daddy, but can you at least leave the door open, so I can see you? Because I'm scared of that window right there." She pointed at the only window in my bedroom.

I nodded and stepped out into the living room, holding Kenosha's face with both of my hands. "What's the matter, baby? Why are you crying?"

She took a deep breath and blinked back tears. "My mother just tried to kill herself again. My aunt just found her in that dope spot over there on 52nd and Sangament. I don't know what to do." She took a step forward and laid her head on my chest, then wrapped her arms around my waist while I rubbed her back.

I never liked to see Kenosha down the way she was. Ever since I had known her she had been going through a bunch of bullshit because of her mother. If it wasn't her going from trap house to trap house looking for her, then it was her mother needing money or damn near overdosing. Janet's drug of choice was crack cocaine, but from time to time she dabbled with that meth shit. Around this time meth was just hitting the hoods of Chicago, and more and more of our people were using it. They said it made them feel as high as crack did, but the high lasted ten times longer.

I brushed her hair out of her face and kissed her on the forehead. "Baby, what do you mean she tried to kill herself? How did she do that?" I tried to imagine Janet jumping off a bridge or something, but I knew it couldn't have been that extreme.

Kenosha came out of my embrace and wrapped her own arms around her body. "She's doing heroin now, and that money I gave her for the rent, she spent it all on that. My aunt was with her the entire night after all that stuff happened with John. She said my mother was shooting large portions of that stuff into her arm, saying she wanted to die. Well, after an hour of doing it, she actually OD'ed and they rushed her to the hospital. She been there since this morning, and I don't know what to do."

I was finding it real hard to feel sorry for her mother because we had been down this road so many times before. I felt it was in her best interest to move on and focus on getting her own life on track. I mean, we had a whole daughter to worry about who needed to be protected by the both of us at all times. I was trying to find a way to let her know how I was feeling without me seeming so insensitive.

She walked into the kitchen and grabbed the box of Popeye's that was on the counter, opened the microwave, and placed it inside after punching in an amount of time for it to warm up. Then she sighed and put her back against the refrigerator, lowering her head. "What should I do, baby?"

I walked up to her and pulled her into my embrace. Her Burberry perfume went up my nose, intoxicating me. She felt soft and womanly in my embrace. Her little arms did their best to wrap around my frame. I lifted her head and kissed her on the lips, sucking them before rubbing the right side of her cheek with my left thumb. "Baby, I'll support you however you need me to. But just in my opinion, I think it's time you release yo' mother and focus more on our daughter and getting your own life on track. You done did all that you can do for her. Now it's time you give yourself a shot and pour that energy into our child and your own future." I kissed her

33

forehead again. "That's just my opinion, though. Like I said before, I'll support you in whatever you decide to do. Now come here."

I pulled her to me again, leaned down, and sucked on her neck before biting right on her thick vein. That shit always drove her crazy. I needed to get her mind off her mother because if she dwelled on Janet's situation too long, it would cause her to go into a deep depression. She struggled with that a lot.

"Mm, baby, stop. I don't feel like that right now. You betta let me go," she said and acted as if she really wanted to push me away.

And I don't know, maybe she did. She had on these real little white biker shorts that looked as if they were painted on. I mean, I could see everything she was working wit' from the waist down, and Kenosha had one of them li'l figures that enticed a man. Every time I really paid attention to what she was working wit', it always brought that animal out of me.

I trailed my big hands down and cupped that ass, squeezing it and biting into her neck. "I know you need me right now, so let me do what I'm supposed to do for my baby." I trailed my hand all the way under them biker shorts until I was rubbing that hot pussy from the back. I could tell she ain't have no panties on because it was scorching, and I could feel her pussy lips clear as day.

"Mm, baby, stop. You already know Madison still woke, so we can't do nothing, anyway. You might as well take these big-ass arms from around me before I get weak. Then we gon' be in trouble."

She moaned and tilted her head back to the ceiling as I slid my hand into her shorts from the back, feeling her hot skin. She spread her legs further and my hand wound up on her naked kitty, stroking, opening and closing her lips between my fingers.

Ski Mask Cartel

I could feel her shake, before groaning deep within her throat as I slid my middle finger deep until her lips wound up on the palm of my hand. "Baby, just come over here and open that refrigerator door real fast. Let me just taste you real fast. Let me make my baby cum for me. I got you."

I didn't even wait for her response. I picked her up into the air and carried her over to the refrigerator and opened the door, praying our daughter didn't come into the kitchen until I got her mother right. As soon as we were where we needed to be in front of it, I opened the door because with the way it opened, as long as Kenosha stayed to the left of it, the door would block off the view from our bedroom or anybody coming from the living room.

Kenosha stood in front of it and pulled her biker shorts all the way down to her ankles and stepped to me as I crouched down in front of her. I gripped her ass in my hands and put my lips right against her pussy, kissing it before opening it up and sliding my tongue in between her crease. She moaned, and I tasted her saltiness, and it drove me crazy. I loved the taste of pussy. To me there was nothing like it.

She reached down and took her shorts all the way off her left foot and opened her thick thighs wide, busting her pussy wide open. "Fuck that, baby. If you gon' eat this shit, then make me cum hard before she come in here. I need you, daddy. Please get me right," she whimpered.

I turned her around and made her bend over, then knelt behind her and sucked her pussy into my mouth, pinching her clit before vacuuming it up loudly. She moaned and opened herself up wider for me. I attacked that kitty like it owed me money, sucking hard on that jewel while I ran three fingers in and out of her.

T.J. Edwards

She bounced back into me, groaning deep within her throat. "Make me cum, baby. Only you can. Please make me cum. I need to so bad. I need you so bad. Uh, uh, please daddy!"

I was slobbering all over that pussy and swallowing as much of her juices as I could, rubbing all over that big ass, just getting as nasty as possible. My baby mother's taste was everything to me. I think I became obsessed with it after she brought my seed into the world, like the birth of our child made me just appreciate her more.

I got to running my fingers in and out of her at full speed and sucking on her clitty so hard I felt like I was gon' pull it off. Her fingers kept on coming back there to help me out, and that turned me on like a muthafucka. She growled and then started to shake like crazy.

She fell to her knees and I pushed her down on the ground and yanked my shorts down, spreading her legs wide open. I had to hit that pussy. I was way too riled up. I just prayed Madison stayed in that room because I needed some of her mother bad.

As soon as I got my dick out, her little hand wrapped around it and she tried to force him into her. I leaned down, lined him up, and slid in while she held her pussy lips apart for me and pulled her tube top up. My baby mother knew I loved to hit that pussy while I sucked on them titties. That shit just went hand-in-hand to me.

As soon as I slammed my way in, I got to killing that shit, trying to get mines while she dug her nails into my back, making her eyes roll to the back of her head. There wasn't nothing like that rushed sex, that kind that parents gotta submit to when they got kids. Sometimes that sex is better than the long, drawn-out kind. I said sometimes.

Luckily Madison fell asleep in my bedroom, so she was oblivious to what we had done in the kitchen.

Chapter 4

The next afternoon, I found myself sitting down on the couch in front of so many assault rifles and handguns I was amazed. Me and Tez had got a call from Rayjon that said we needed to meet him at his crib over on 72nd and Bishop. That is the south side of Chicago. The area is infested with Gangster Disciples, and niggas don't like nobody that ain't plugged with their mob.

As soon as Rayjon texted me the information of where he stayed and that he wanted to meet there, I was skeptical about going. Back in the day me and Tez had robbed a couple niggas a few blocks over on Marshfield, and just like the Holy City hit on the west side a few days ago, we neglected to use masks. We didn't know if we had waiting enemies for us over there or not, but just as usual Tez convinced me to go by reminded me Rayjon promised us 50 thousand dollars apiece.

That was all the incentive I needed. I had a full plate of people who depended on me. I had to find a crib for my baby mother and daughter out of the hood, and I wanted to be able to pay up at least six months' worth of rent. On top of that, I made sure I paid my mother's rent every month, and I had been doing it ever since I was sixteen years old. I was sure she could've handled it on her own, but I refused to let that happen. I felt like I owed her for being a single mother and raising me and my sister on her own.

My father was given life in prison when I was just six years old. He'd bodied three niggas over in Gary, Indiana over $1,000,000 they stole from him. Our relationship wasn't the strongest because of the distance in between, but I held a deep respect for the man just because he was my father. I kept his books straight always and drove my mother out to see him twice a month.

T.J. Edwards

Rayjon handed me an AK-47 and a banana clip. I slammed the clip into the bottom of the rifle and cocked it. It felt heavy in my hands, but it sure was pretty, all black with a scope on top of it. I was already imagining a few niggas I could body with it.

I looked across from me as Tez was handed a black-and-gold one that looked just like the ones them muthafuckas in the Middle East carried. He had his tongue out of his mouth and looked excited. "Jo, who we finna hit with these muthafuckas? I mean, I don't care who it is. I'm just ready to see what kind of damage this bitch do." He aimed it across the small apartment and smiled.

Niggas in Chicago have a habit of started their sentences with the word Jo or ending them that way. Jo isn't a person, it's just how we talk. My cousin got that shit bad, so from time to time I'd see him saying that shit.

Rayjon sat down on the loveseat and pulled a fat ass blunt out of a box of Garcia Vegas on the glass table in front of us. "Before I even came to this city, a few muthafuckas I rotate with and trust with my life put me up on game for a few licks to get my feet wet. I'm talking connects that are the connects to the muthafuckas we finna hit. I know what everybody got and where it's supposed to go." He took the blunt, lit the tip, and passed it to Tez before doing the same thing twice more, making it so we all had a fat ass blunt of Dro.

I took four strong pulls and inhaled deeply. Weed always made me focus in on every word being said. I could even put pictures to 'em. I needed to see where this nigga was going wit' shit before I jumped down wit' him.

Rayjon took a pull off his blunt and inhaled the smoke. "Y'all remember I said I was gon' put fifty gees apiece in yo' pockets, right?"

Me and Tez nodded in unison. I was listening like my life depended on it. I already had that fifty spent in my head. I had to get my people right, and that would be a nice first step.

Rayjon stood up, and I noted he was wearing a bulletproof vest under his black wife-beater. He walked into the kitchen while me and Tez continued to blow our Dro. When he came back into the front room, he had a carton of orange juice open and was drinking from it. "The niggas we hitting tonight got a safe that should have no less than two hundred gees. We just gon' have to work a li'l bit to get to it."

He took another sip and swallowed loudly. I watched his adam's apple move up and down. Every time he swallowed, I could hear that shit. That was weird to me.

"Now, me personally, I fuck wit' these hammers, but I like to slice a muthafucka open, so I can let them see they self bleed slowly. The pain is intensified. The niggas we gon' hit tonight gon' be caught slipping because I got a few bitches in place that pledge they allegiance to this Ski Mask way of life. It's a li'l get-together that's taking place honoring this nigga by the name of Colly. A li'l orgy of sorts. While these niggas fucking, we gon' go from room to room knocking they ass off until we get to Colly himself, and I'm gon' have him open the safe and give us what we came for. Now, the connects I'm fucking wit' don't care about what's in that safe. They care about this nigga losing his life, along with us making a statement. Y'all handle ya business and leave the payouts to me. Honor me as head and we can set this Cartel in stone right now." He looked at Tez, then back over to me.

Just being honest, I really didn't care about killing a bunch of niggas if it meant at the end of it all I was gon' be able to provide for my people. Far as I was concerned, Rayjon could have lined them up and I would've knocked them down with no hesitation, and I was pretty

T.J. Edwards

sure Tez was feeling the same way. I didn't know why Rayjon chose me and my cousin to go on this move wit' him instead of other niggas he was already down wit', so I asked him that. "Say, big homie, why you choosing us to handle this bitness wit' instead of some of them other niggas I know you fuckin' wit'? How you know we gon' hold you down like we supposed to?"

Rayjon shrugged his shoulders. "I really don't, but I been hearin' about that nigga Tez ever since he got Raven pregnant, and she say he's a savage. She already know how I get down, so if she lumping us in the same category, then I gotta see what that look like with the both of us on a lick. Now, far as you go, I lost my brother a few months back to the gun. Before he passed away, he was the only nigga I would hit licks wit' because he got down just like I did. Real killas know other killas, and most killas choose to ride alone unless they know that the nigga they riding wit' is just like them. So, when I look at Tez, it's just like I'm looking at you when it comes to this Ski Mask shit, and vice versa."

To me the homie was making sense, and I ain't feel like questioning him no further, especially since Tez had his face scrunched up and was giving me a look that said he didn't want me to fuck this up for us.

Tez dumped his ashes into the ashtray before standing up and giving Rayjon a half-hug. "Nigga, I pledge my loyalty to you and honor you as chief of this Ski Mask Cartel that you building wit' us. As long as you keep me eating, I'll keep that gun busting for you, and them knives digging a nigga's heart out." He paused and smiled. "Shid, bitches, too, if it come to that. I ain't gender prejudice."

Before it was all said and done, I got up and pledged my loyalties to the homie, too. I was ready to get my bands all the way up, and if I had to shed a little blood,

Ski Mask Cartel

I was all for it just as long as at the end of it all I could feed my people.

***

A little after eleven that same night, it started to snow in Chicago like crazy. It felt like it came out of nowhere because the day before it had been a li'l sunny and fair, but this night the snow was falling from the sky in big flakes.

Rayjon pulled the van into the alley and shut the engine off. Out my window I could see the snow was already starting to stick to the ground. Two big-ass rats were running down the dark alley. chasing a cat that had patches of its fur missing. There was one light that illuminated where we were, but it was blinking on and off. A little ways down the alley, I could see a few people standing in front of a metal garbage can that had a fire going inside of it. I kind of worried about them being there, seeing as what we were getting ready to do.

Tez cocked his .45 and put it back into his waistband, then did the same thing with his .44 Desert Eagle. "Jo, you think I should run down the alley real fast and body them burns before we even go in here?" he asked, looking down the alley with a mug on his face.

Rayjon looked out of his windshield and shook his head. "Nah, kid, fuck them burns. We trying to make this shit happen inside of this house so we don't end up like them. They good. If shit change, I'll handle them on my own," he assured and cocked his guns back. He was dressed in black army fatigues. The inside of his jacket, I noted, was lined with a few knives I'd seen him load up with. "Yo, Racine. You good back there, my nigga?"

I nodded. "Yeah, I'm just ready to kick this shit off so we can get this bread. But I'm good, though." Even though I told him that, I had to admit to myself I was a little worried about what we were finna get into. Most niggas jack and front like every time they hit a lick they didn't get scared or worried, but that was bullshit. Well, at least for me. I was 'bout that action, but at the same time I had so much common sense that at times it got the better of me. I always felt like anything could go wrong at any time. Then Madison always came to my mind, followed by Kenosha.

Rayjon's phone vibrated. He looked down at it and nodded his head, texting something back that I couldn't see. "Yo, that's my inside connect right there. She ready for us and gon' meet us at the back door. Remember, Racine, you gon' take the two rooms that's in the basement. It's gon' be two niggas fucking the same ho. You body both them niggas and that bitch. Tez, you gon' go to the first floor and hit them two room. It's gon' be a fat nigga in one fucking with two hos, and in the other one a li'l skinny nigga that look just like him 'cuz it's his son. He gon' have one bitch with him. Everybody gotta go. Those are the orders. This is where I see how you niggas get down. Leave the upstairs to me, and the muthafuckas up there. A'ight?"

I nodded and saw Tez do the same. I was wondering how we was finna go in there and get to busting and shit without them niggas reacting and returning fire before we could make it to our second destination. I guess I would just have to figure shit out as I went along.

I rolled down my mask and adjusted my vest on my chest that Rayjon had provided. It was my first time wearing one, and it was real heavy. It felt like it was at least fifteen pounds.

Ten minutes later we were crouched down at the back door of this brown duplex. The snow was really coming down now, and it was real windy. It's like the wind was blowing that shit into my eyes on purpose. I kept on blinking, and I felt my shit running like crazy.

Ski Mask Cartel

In the distance I could hear the burns down the alley laughing about somethin', and once again them being there worried me.

The back door opened, scaring the shit out of me because it caught me off guard. I upped my pistol and everything, ready to blow some shit back, and I couldn't help but see Madison's face in my mind's eye. I had to make it back to my baby. I had to get this shit over and done with.

A female stood in the doorway, damn near naked if not for the purple bra and panties she had on that barely covered her body. As soon as she opened the door, the wind hit her, and she shielded herself behind the door.

"Everything in place, baby. Go handle yo' bitness." She said this to Rayjon before stepping out into the cold with a little purse in her hand. The last I saw of her, she was running toward the alley where we had come from.

Rayjon nodded his head hard. "Let's make this shit happen, bruh. Loyalty, niggas." He rushed into the house through the back door, followed by Tez, followed by me.

As soon as I stepped in, the heat enveloped me. That and the strong smell of sex. I mean it smelt like everybody in that house was fucking in front of a fan, because it was loud. That and the music. After I heard how loud everything was, I got to worrying about the neighbors. Like I said before, I got too much common sense.

I ran down the stairs into the basement. It was dark, and I couldn't really see shit other than light coming from under a door a few paces ahead. I took that to be the room the threesome was fucking in. I stopped right outside of it and put my ear to the door. I could hear a bunch of huffing and puffing along with the squeaking of a bed. I remembered he said it was two rooms down there, so since I knew there was fucking in the room I was standing in front of, I thought it would be in my best interest to locate the other room just to make sure nobody was in.

I jogged away from the door and went all the way to the back of the basement where I guessed the other room would be. Most duplexes were set up the same way in Chicago. Sure enough, there was another room, and to my horror there was a female crouched down on her knees throwing up inside of a garbage can. The room was dark with the only light coming from the small television. I stepped to the side of the door, out of her view, with my stomach turning upside down. I hated killing women. I always tried to make that my last resort. Fuck, I wished she didn't have to be there at that time.

She finished puking into the garbage can, then lay across the bed with her face sideways on the pillow. I could tell she was sick because she kept on groaning before curling herself into a ball on the bed. I shook my head and said fuck killing her. She was already going through enough pain in my mind. I saw Kenosha's face and imagined her being at the wrong place at the wrong time and some nigga killing her for nothing, and that shit made me feel sick a little bit.

Before I could talk myself out of it, I ran in the room and jumped on her back, wrapping my arm under her chin and applying pressure. I wasn't trying to kill her, just put her ass to sleep. She struggled against me and tried to shake herself loose, freaking out. I could hear her screaming deep within her throat while she kicked her legs.

I tightened my grip and prayed she calmed down or I was gon' have to really body her ass, and I ain't wanna do that. I slid off the bed and held her in the air. Her feet kicked wildly as I maintained the pressure under her chin as her resistance got weaker and weaker until, finally, she passed out and I laid her across the bed, feeling the sweat saturate my mask.

Ski Mask Cartel

I stepped out of the room and heard muffled booms upstairs. That let me know either Tez or Rayjon was up there on bitness. I took my .40 Glock out of my waistband and ran back in front of the door I had previously been in front of when I first came into the basement. I took a step back and kicked the door in with all my might. *Whoom!*

It flew open to reveal a big screen television with a porno playing on the screen. In the bed was a muscular black nigga about my size and a li'l skinny dude with short corn rows. It seemed like both niggas damn near broke their necks to get to the dresser, where there was a 9-millimeter on top of it. The muscular nigga had been between the female's legs, but when that door kicked in he pulled out of her and dove for the dresser's top where the gun was located. The li'l skinny nigga tried to jump across the bed to get there first, and I hit his ass up wit' no mercy while the female dropped to the floor and rolled under the bed, screaming.

Boom! Boom! Boom! Three bullets lit up the skinny nigga's back and threw him forward into the wall, where he crashed before sinking to the carpet in slow motion.

The muscular nigga grabbed the gun, dropped to the floor, and turned around busting. *Boom! Boom! Boom! Boom! Boom! Boom! Boom! Boom! Boom!*

I dropped down to the floor. What the fuck was wrong wit' this nigga? He was literally busting back-to-back, and most of his bullets were hitting the ceiling, knocking chunks out of it. I put my back against the doorframe and continued to let him do him while the broad screamed under the bed like somebody was killing her.

Boom! Boom! Boom! Boom! He kept spitting until suddenly, he wasn't. I figured that shit out right away: that nigga was busting a 9mm. He must've only had thirteen shots. Boy, was I happy about that.

T.J. Edwards

I jumped up after I heard him in there throwing open the dresser drawers. I guessed he was looking for more bullets. I ran into the room and aimed right at his naked back.

Boom! Boom! Boom! "Bitch-ass nigga."

"*Ahhh!*" he hollered, arching his back. Then he turned around and faced me. I noted the bullets had ripped through him and caused three big-ass holes to appear in his upper stomach and chest. He was bleeding profusely, yet he still rushed me at full speed, nearly catching me off guard.

Boom! Boom! Boom! Boom! Boom! His body jumped backward as hole after hole appeared in his chest before he fell to his knees with his eyes wide open. The room smelled like gunpowder and my ears were ringing from the loud shots. My heart was beating hard in my chest.

The female sounded like she was becoming hysterical under the bed. I could hear her screaming and making weird noises just as Tez appeared behind me, almost giving me a heart attack.

"Nigga, you good down here?" he hollered, putting his hand on my back and looking at the two dead niggas.

"Yeah, fool. It's just a female under the bed, but she ain't no threat. I done already murked them niggas, so let's go." I turned, headed for the stairs.

"Hell nall!" I heard Tez say, making me stop in my tracks. "That nigga Rayjon say kill everybody, nigga, so that's what we gotta do. Where this bitch at?" he growled.

She screamed, and I watched him flip the bed with one hand, first the mattress, and then the box spring, exposing the naked female who was curled into a ball with snot running from her nose.

46

"Please don't kill me! Please, I swear, I'll never say nothing. I'm only seventeen years old. Please!" she begged.

Now I was really feeling some type of way about killing her. I grabbed Tez's arm. "Yo, fuck her, man. Let's go, cuz. She ain't no threat."

Tez jerked away from me. "Nall, fuck that, nigga. This bitch ain't gon' fuck my paper up. Say yo' prayers, shorty." He aimed the gun right at her and pulled the trigger, lighting her up. *Boom! Boom! Boom! Boom! Boom! Boom!*

Her body jumped up and down as it filled up wit' holes. I felt horrible. I hoped the other broad didn't wake up and come out of the room or I knew he was gon' kill her, too. But, thankfully, she never did.

Rayjon came down to the basement with a black garbage bag. "Yo, kid, it's time to ride out. Mission accomplished."

T.J. Edwards

Chapter 5

Three weeks later Kenosha finally found a nice li'l crib to move into out in Riverdale. Riverdale is the suburb of Chicago where the population is basically mixed in with all races of people. The houses are nice, and since the crib was in the suburbs, I really didn't have to worry about too much bad shit happening to her and my daughter, although my ultimate goal was to be able to move them out of Chicago, period. I wanted my li'l family to be able to live safely and in the lap of luxury, and if I had anything to say about it, I was gon' make it happen one day.

In that same week, Rayjon had kept his word and blessed me and Tez wit' fifty gees apiece. Once I got the money in hand, my first order of bitness was making sure Kenosha's rent was paid up for six months. Then I took her to the car lot and leased her a nice li'l 2019 Audi she went crazy over. I knew her favorite color was pink, so I figured I'd get it changed from the black color we'd got it in to pink later down the road. I wanted to buy the whip right out, but they wanted 35 bands for it, that would have eaten up all the li'l bread that I'd just made, so we got the car note and I paid it up for six months after the initial down payment of three gees.

After we left the lot, we hit up the furniture store and got her right in that department. Then it was time for the mall. It had been a short while since I had been in a position to really let her pick out some shit I knew she'd really like

I spent ten gees on just her outfits, and another five on my daughter. I ain't really worry about me because they were more important. I figured I would think about myself after our next lick, which Rayjon promised would be a little more to split.

T.J. Edwards

I just liked to see them running around the mall and picking out whatever they wanted. It made me feel good. Providing was everything to me. I felt like they shouldn't have had to worry about nothing in life other than being happy. As a man, I felt it was my job to provide for both of them in every single way, from my daughter on up to Kenosha, whom I honored because she had brought my child into this world. For that blessing alone, I would always feel indebted to her.

Around seven o'clock that night I rang the doorbell to my mother's crib, and she answered it with a big smile on her face.

"Hey, baby. It's about time you got here. I didn't think you was gon' show up. You know how you do," she said, pursing her lips to help shoot the slug she'd shot at me.

I pulled her into my embrace and wrapped my arms around her as the wind picked up and the snow brushed across my back. I kissed her cheek. "I told you I was coming. My word is always one hunnit when it comes to you."

I felt Madison's little hands trying to pull me away from her grandma. "Grandma, it's cold out here. Can't we go inside your hot house now?" she asked with her brown nose turning a shade of pink.

My mother, Lin, knelt down and picked her up into her arms, walking with her into the house. "Oh, baby, I missed you so much. I ain't seen you in three days. That's too long for my baby to be away from me." She started to kiss all over Madison's cheeks, and I got a little jealous because I didn't like nobody kissing all over my daughter if it wasn't me.

Kenosha came up behind me and wrapped her arms around my waist. "Come on, baby. Let's get some of this heat. Plus, I wanna see what yo' momma cooked. She always throwing down on somethin'," she said, walking into the house before stepping to the side and taking her Steve Madden Ugg boots off. I stepped in and removed my Timms as the aroma of all kinds of food hit my nostrils and made me smile.

My mom was the type of old school woman who kept all her sofas in plastic. Her crib was decked out from top to bottom with her own unique style. She was originally from the south, so she had a thing for wicker chairs. Even though she upgraded her furniture every few years, it seemed like she made it a point to never get rid of the old wicker chairs. I had grown up with them in the house, and I found them to be a little comfortable, at least more comfortable than the plastic-covered couches that were in the living room, so I plopped down into one of the chairs and Kenosha sat on my lap.

"Momma, what you in there throwing down on?" Kenosha asked, wigglin' around a little bit to get herself comfortable on my lap. Once that big ass was perfectly centered, she leaned backward until her back was up against my chest. I brushed her microbraids out of my face before kissing her on the neck. I could smell the coconut oil she used in her hair, along with her perfume. I liked her scents.

My mother came into the living room and put Madison down, then handed her a tablet she'd brought for her to use whenever she came over to her house. Madison wandered off into the front room and disappeared. "I got some fried chicken, collard greens, white rice, pinto beans, cornbread, and for dessert I made a German chocolate cake. I been preparing for y'all to get here ever since yesterday." She smiled, showing off the dimples that accentuated both of her round cheeks.

My mother was a small woman of about five-foot-three and maybe weighed 115 pounds. She wore glasses and her favorite designer was Dolce and Gabanna. She was deeply religious and didn't play about her Jesus.

As soon as she left to go into the kitchen, Kenosha jumped off my lap, turned around, and kissed my lips. "Baby, I wish my mother was like yours. You ain't never gotta worry about what dope house you gon' find Lin in. She love God too much. My mother got me feeling sick as hell right now. I still don't know what to do."

I stood up and wrapped her in my arms, holding her tight. "Baby, like I said before, whatever you wanna do regarding yo' mother, I got yo' back one hunnit percent. You ain't never gotta worry about doing nothing alone. I got you. You understand that?"

She looked up at me and smiled. I could tell she was touched by how I was coming at her, but everything I told her, I meant. I never wanted her to feel alone in anything or any situation in the world. I felt like it was my job to be there for her in every way I could be.

After we threw down on the food my mother whipped, Kenosha and Madison went into my mother's guest room and lay down to take a nap, I'm guessing because they ate so much. I stayed in the kitchen and helped my mother do the dishes. I always liked helping her do that. I don't know why for certain, I guess it was simply my need to be close to the queen who gave birth to me and my way of showing her my appreciation for all she was in my life. I felt most niggas let the streets make them forget it was okay to be soft sometimes, especially when you had women in the family who needed that emotional maleness. I loved my mother with all of my heart, and when I found windows to be able to bond wit' her, I took them and made the best of them.

After we finished with the dishes, I pulled her into the front room and pulled out five gees, in all hunnits, and handed it to her. "Here, Ma. This for the rent and whatever other bills you got for this month. I'm trying to bust a few moves, so I can help you hit my pop's books next week, too, so don't even worry about that."

Ski Mask Cartel

She took the money and fanned it out in her face. "Boy, now I know dang well you ain't got no job, yet every month you always handing me piles of money. Should I ask where you getting it from?" She adjusted her glasses on her nose and put her hand on her hip, her salt-and-pepper curls falling across her chest.

I shook my head. "You the one person in this world I ain't never lied too ever since I was a kid. I don't wanna start that habit now." I took the money from her and put it into a knot, then gave it back to her. "I'm in the streets, Momma, and right now it's the only way I know how to provide. I know it ain't right, but it's the truth. And before you even get started, it ain't got nothing to do with the way you raised me, because you raised me in church and I know better. But it's just in me to make things happen for this family. I hold what the Bible says about First Timothy 5:8 real close to my heart." I brushed her curls out of her face as she looked up at me.

She took a deep breath and exhaled slowly, then a small smile came across her face. "You always been a man, even when you were a kid. You always found a way to bring momma some kind of money. I never understood how you were like that so young, but I'll tell you what, it made me proud." Her smile grew wider. She reached and pinched my cheek. "Son, I know what you out there doing in them streets ain't right, but your intentions are pure, and I get that. And I know I could stand here and try to preach the word of God to you until I'm blue in the face, but I know that, in the end, you're going to probably make the same choices, so I'll refrain from doing that. What I will say is I love you, baby, and I want you to be careful because I need you, and so do those girls in that other room. Especially Madison. Always keep that at the forefront of your mind, and please be smart. That's all I ask as your mother. Now come here," she said, stepping forward and hugging me tight. "Thank you, son. I never worry about anything, and it's all because of you."

We stayed up and chatted for another hour before Kenosha wandered out of the room and found us sitting in the front room, laughing and reminiscing about when I was a shorty. My mother seemed like she didn't forget nothing I did, and it was crazy to me.

"Baby, I miss you. I need for you to come and hold me, so I can fall into a deep sleep," Kenosha said, looking at me with them pretty brown eyes that drove me crazy.

My mother looked over at her and smiled before standing up and yawning. "I'll tell y'all what, I'll go into the guest room and sleep with Madison. That way y'all can have some alone time downstairs in the den. I know it's probably been a while since y'all had any."

I swear, I don't even think she got that full sentence out of her mouth before we were downstairs, and I had Kenosha's knees pressed to her chest, eating that pussy good. I made her hold the back of her thighs wide. I opened her kitty up and sucked on each individual lip, before sticking my tongue as far as it could go into her.

"Mm, daddy, yeah! Get that pussy, daddy. Please, get that pussy, daddy. Please! Ah!" she moaned with her mouth wide open, her pussy juices oozing out of her.

I peeled her lips back a little further until her clit popped all the way out. As soon as I saw it, I trapped it and sucked on it like I was trying to give it a hickey. Kenosha jerked around on the bed and let her thighs go. She humped into my face and wrapped her ankles around my neck.

"Yes, daddy. Yes! Please, oh yes, baby. Uh. Uh. I'm cumming!" she screamed, shaking on the bed like she was having a seizure.

I kept on licking and sucking, rubbing her pussy all over my face, getting as nasty as possible. I loved how her pussy tasted. It drove me crazy for some reason.

She came again, screaming into a pillow, then I picked her little ass up and threw her on her stomach on the bed. I pushed her right knee to her ribs, took my dick head, and pushed him in with authority. Her hot pussy seared me, her grip was tight, and I had to roll my eyes backward before I grabbed a handful of her hair, yanking her head backward, plunging into that shit like I was mad at her. "This my pussy, baby. Tell daddy this his pussy right now or I'm gon' bust this shit open! Tell me!" I demanded, slamming into her so hard it sounded like I was smacking her on her naked back.

Her pussy was making wet, squishing sounds that were driving me nuts. Every time my dick drove forward, it made that sound, and it caused me to cock back and ram it even harder. "This my daddy's pussy. This yo' pussy, daddy. I swear to God it is. Mm, just keep hitting it like you doing. I love it so much! Aw daddy!" she screamed and bit back into the pillow.

I felt her shaking, grabbed her by the hair, and pulled her up to all fours and really got to long-stroking that pussy. All the way back, then slamming forward with authority. Any time I got inside of my baby mother, I made sure I put my name inside of that ass.

I got to rocking her at full speed as I felt my nut building up. The headboard rocked against the wall. I could smell our scent in the air. She moaned loudly into the pillow and slamming her ass back into my lap, and it was all too much. I saw that big booty jiggle a few times, and then I let that cum fly deep into her womb while I kept going in and out of her. I rubbed all over that ass as her walls milked me. Afterward she pulled me out of her and sucked both of our juices off him

T.J. Edwards
while looking me in the eye and telling me how much
she loved me.

Chapter 6

The next day it was snowing so bad outside I didn't even wanna leave the house. I hated that kind of weather. I personally didn't like the cold. I was more of a spring type of nigga because I really didn't like the heat, either. I think it had something to do wit' the fact I was born in April, which is in the spring.

Rayjon hit my phone and said he wanted us to meet up at the Homerun Inn over on the east side. I wanted to tell him I didn't fuck wit' the cold, but then he said the meeting was in the interest of more than before, which I took to mean he had a lick that was gon' gross more than fifty stacks, so I was all for it.

An hour later I was sitting across from him and my cousin with a meat lover's pizza in front of us. I really ain't have no appetite at first, but when I saw both niggas going to town on the pizza it made me want to check it out, and boy was I glad I did because that muthafucka was lit.

Rayjon wiped his mouth on a napkin and took a sip from the glass of Pepsi. "This time we finna hit up some Mexicans out west." He took a long sip from the pop and then sat the glass back on the table after burping and hitting his chest. "Fuck. Anyway, the reason we hitting these niggas up is because they just got a shipment of assault rifles in, and the muthafucka who sold it to 'em want them pieces back. And they gon' give us half of the money."

Tez frowned, and I did the same thing because that didn't sound right to me. "Bro, what you mean they sold them the weapons, but they want them back? That don't make sense to me," I said, setting my slice of pizza back on my plate.

Tez didn't give a fuck and talked with a mouth full of food. I could barely understand what he was saying. "Yeah, bruh. You gotta explain that shit to us a little better than what you doing."

Rayjon nodded his head. "Cool. Look, it's like I told you li'l homies before, I got connects that get down how they get down. Now, one of my connects just sold a shipment of assault rifles to these Mexicans out west. The Mexicans paid them a hunnit and eighty bands for the crate of choppahs. All we gotta do it hit they ass and return the crate, then my connect gon' hit our hands wit' 90 gees and a few pieces from the crate. The job shouldn't take us more than ten minutes to complete because they keep the crate in the back of their tattoo parlor on Spaulding and Potomac."

Now I knew this nigga was tripping. "Bruh, you talking about going into Humboldt Park and fucking wit' them *eses* for ninety gees? That's right in the heart of Cobra land. This Mexicans over there about that action, fo' real, and ninety gees ain't worth losing our lives for," I said, thinking about everything my mother had told me the day before.

Tez nodded. "Yeah, I gotta agree wit' my cousin here, big homie. You break that ninety down three ways, that's only thirty gees apiece. Last move we pulled got us fifty, and it was far less danger. The *eses* looney over there, and then muthafuckas racist. I don't even know how we would get in there to begin with," he said, lowering his head as if he were in deep thought.

Rayjon curled his lip as if he was getting angry, and I didn't give no fuck. I was ready to get into it wit' that nigga over this. I knew how them Mexican cats got down in Humboldt Park, and they didn't play no games. They were extreme gangbangers, and deadly. All it would take is us to make one false move and we'd all be dead. That nigga Rayjon was from New Jersey somewhere. I don't think he really knew how mutha-fuckas in Chicago got down in the slums.

He exhaled slowly. "A'ight, on this move you nig-gas can keep the money, and I'll just take the dope that's gon' be in there." He took out a toothpick and started to mess wit' his teeth, sucking on them loudly and annoy-ingly. I hated when people did that.

Tez perked up. "Wait, you ain't say shit about no dope. How much is we talking, and what kind?" His eyes were bucked wide open as if he were intrigued.

Rayjon sat back and smiled. "Yeah, I knew that would get yo' attention. You niggas didn't even let me finish. It's gon' be five bricks of heroin in there. That tar shit, street value seventy-five thousand apiece. I was gon' make it to where you niggas got thirty gees and a brick of tar apiece. That's a hunnit and five gees right there."

Tez nodded his head hard. "Fuck that, I'm in. I don't give a fuck what we gotta do. I'm in, my nigga. What about you, Racine?"

I exhaled and slowly nodded. There wasn't no way I was passing up a hunnit and five stacks. That was good money, and with the plate I had, it was much needed.

Rayjon saw my response and his face turned serious. "A'ight, well, we gon' hit they ass at three in the morn-ing, right before they close that tattoo parlor. I got an inside connect that own the bar next to the shop. We gon' utilize his establishment to make this happen."

***

I strolled back to my mother's crib because that's where Kenosha and Madison were chilling. The weather was too bad for Kenosha to be driving in it, plus she didn't trust her own driving skills, no way. Usually be-fore a lick I would chill wit' Tez and smoke blunt after blunt until we got ready to handle business, and I planned on doing that, but I was missing my daughter like crazy and it was getting the better of me.

After I took my Timms off at the door, she ran to me screaming "Daddy!" all loud and stuff, and I picked her up and wrapped my arms around her before kissing all over her little brown, soft cheeks.

"Daddy, I missed you all day. You was gon' too long," she said, hugging me tight.

I carried her toward the guest room, speaking to my mother and Kenosha as I passed. They were in the kitchen talking about something I couldn't put together. When I got to the guest room, I closed the door and sat my daughter down on the edge of the bed and knelt in front of her, grabbing her little hands. "Baby, I just want you to know I love you and you are really, really special to me. Do you understand that, princess?"

She nodded her head, and the braids Kenosha had put in her hair that morning shook back and forth with the barrettes on the ends of them. They were black and white to match her new Prada dress I had bought her. It made her look so beautiful.

"I love you, too, Daddy. Are you gonna play dolls wit' me?" she asked, turning her head to the side.

I smiled and held her hands a li'l more firmly. "Baby, I just want you to listen to me, and then we can play. Okay?"

She nodded. "'Kay, Daddy."

I took a deep breath. "Baby, I love you and you are really special to me. I am proud to be your daddy, and I am happy you are my daughter. You are very beautiful, and you are the best baby girl in the whole wide world. I will do anything for you, forever. Come here." I stood up and picked her up, just holding my baby girl, feeling her little arms wrap around me. I felt like I needed the strength she rendered onto me. I needed to feel my purpose in life, because a part of me was a little leery about messing with them *eses*. I got to worrying about not making it back to my kid, and that made me sick to the stomach.

I set Madison down on her two feet and looked into her brown eyes, rubbing her cheek with my thumb. "You're perfect, baby. Now let's play wit' your toys. I'm here for you."

***

By three in the morning, the wind was blowing so hard my eyes were frozen. I had to keep on closing them, and every time I opened them frost would fly right back into them. I was freezin' like a muthafucka, too, because it was cold outside. And there I was, jogging down an alley with the wind blowing like crazy, only dressed in black True Religion jeans, a bulletproof vest with a black polo sweater over it, Timms, and a black ski mask. I had a big-ass five-shot Masburg pump wit' me, too. I was ready to put some holes in somethin'.

I was thankful it was freezing the way it was outside because I didn't see anybody out other than me and Tez as we ran down the alley and into the back of the bar Rayjon said his connect owned. When we got to the back door, Rayjon was holding it open with his mask rolled up his face as if it were a regular skullcap.

He put his arm out, blocking us from coming inside. "Look, y'all roll them masks up before y'all come in or y'all gon' spook this nigga and his bitch in here," he said, looking over his shoulder as the wind blew against my back.

I rolled my mask up and watched Tez do the same thing. Now that was done, I wondered what I was supposed to do about the big-ass Masburg I was carrying.

Tez had a DSK that spit fifty rounds. His weapon wasn't as long as mine, but it was just as chunky.

I held my shit in front of Rayjon face. "Nigga, if they worried about masks, what we gon' do about these?" I said, freezing like a muthafucka. Even though my hands were in black leather gloves, they still felt numb.

He shook his head. "You know what? Fuck it. I'm killing them anyway. Those were my orders. Y'all come on." He waved us inside.

I was thankful for the heat as soon as it came over me, but the bar smelled like a mildewed mop head. That shit was horrible.

We came in through the back way, right into a little kitchen that had roaches crawling all around in a frenzy. There was a sink with a few plates in it filled up with dirty water, and the water had at least eight dead roaches in it. The floor was caked up with dried mud and black shoe prints. The small white stove looked like somebody had been cooking some kind of sauce in a pot, but it overflowed and spilled over the sides of the stove and the people just left it to dry. Big-ass cockroaches were huddled around the dried-up stuff, I guessed eating from it. When I saw two rats run across the floor, I jumped and then shook my head. These folks were gross, and I made a note to never come to this bar.

We went through another door and entered the front of the bar where there was an older Mexican man and a younger twenty-something female sitting at a table with their eyes pinned on a television closer to the ceiling. When we came through the door, they looked over at us for a brief second and then went right back to watching the flat screen.

The bar looked like a normal tavern. There was nothing special or different about it except the nasty-ass kitchen and the fact it smelled like ass and dirty mop water.

Ski Mask Cartel

Rayjon pointed at a table. "Look, kid, y'all sit over there and watch how I get down for this paper."

I shrugged my shoulders and was happy to pop a squat. My toes were frozen along with my fingers, and I was hoping it took him a short while to handle his business.

Tez sat across from me and crinkled his nose. "Jo, it stank like a muthafucka in here. Did you peep they kitchen? Ugh!"

I laughed a li'l bit because that's exactly how I was feeling. Even though the li'l Mexican chick sitting at the front of the bar looked fine as hell, I thought she was gross just because of how the bar looked and smelled. "Yeah, bruh. They nasty as a muthafucka in here."

I watched Rayjon walk right in front of the older Mexican man before pausing in front of him and talking with his hands. I couldn't hear what he was saying, but all the sudden he grabbed the fat man by the face with one of his big hands, pulled a blade from his waist, and got to slicing him across the face again and again so fast that before I realized what he was doing, he had already sliced him five times, still going.

The female jumped up from her chair and screamed. He punched her so hard she flew backward and fell sideways onto the floor with her left leg kicking. Then he grabbed the older man, who was now on the floor crawling around with blood skeeting from his face, by the hair and slammed him on top of the table furthest away from us. This made me get up and run to his side with my Masburg exposed.

"Uh! Uh! Please, man. Okay, I'll give you what you want, son. You don't have to kill me or my wife," he stammered.

Rayjon pulled him from the table and slammed the knife into his shoulder after putting his hand over the man's mouth. "Bitch-ass nigga. I told you to stop

63

playing wit' me. I wouldn't be here unless I knew for a fact you had them birds in this muthafucka. Now take me to that safe in the back. I ain't got time for this shit." He pushed the man so hard he fell onto his knees.

The man looked up at him with his bottom lip quivering. "Pablo said you were coming as a friend. He said your target was the people next door. Why are you doing this to us?"

Rayjon picked him up and pulled the knife out of his shoulder.

"Ah! Fucking A! Okay, man," he hollered, jumping up. "Follow me," he said with blood gushing out of his shoulder. His face looked like a mess. Gashes were everywhere. Blood dripped off his chin and ran down his chest, saturating his shirt.

Rayjon looked down at the broad who was laid flat out on the floor. "Say, kid. One of you niggas kill that bitch before she wake up. If this old geezer don't give me what I came for, I'm gon' kill his ass, too. Word is bond." He snatched him up by the shirt and threw him in front of him. "Bring yo' ass on."

As Rayjon left, Tez ran over to my side with the DSK in his hand. "Jo, that nigga Rayjon is a goon. You see how he cut that old man up and knocked this punkass bitch out? Damn! That's that gangsta shit right there," he said, real giddy.

I personally didn't give a fuck how Rayjon was getting down, and in my eyes, it wasn't that hard to slice up an old man and knock out a female, especially if he caught them off guard like he did. I just wasn't impressed. I was wondering why we was in a bar slicing muthafuckas up when the real money was supposed to be in the tattoo shop. That was throwing me for a loop.

I heard the old man cry out in the back of the bar somewhere at the same time the bitch on the floor started to move.

Ski Mask Cartel

Tez didn't waste no time as her knelt beside her, pressing his DSK to her forehead. I saw his finger go to the trigger before I pulled his arm away. "Nigga, that's a loud-ass gun. What if them muthafuckas hear it next door and leave? Or even worse, call the police or somethin'?" I said, looking at him like he had lost his fucking mind.

The female opened her eyes wide and started to scoot backward on her ass before making a weird-ass noise deep within her throat. "Please, don't kill me. I'm sorry. I don't know anything. I swear."

She looked around in a panic before Tez ran over and grabbed her by the hair aggressively, mugging the shit out of me. The female started to claw at his hands to break his hold, but he didn't seem to pay her no mind. He kept his eyes pinned on me.

"Cuz, this bitch gotta die, just like big homie said. Damn, nigga, what is it wit' you and killin' hos? This shit ain't that hard."

He gripped her skinny neck with his fingers, squeezing tightly, cutting off her air supply. She tried to dislodge his hand from around her throat and continued to struggle against his grip, using her last breath to scream for help. When she finally stopped moving, he let her limp body fall to the ground.

All I could do was shake my head. *Damn! Another innocent female at the wrong place at the wrong time.*

Rayjon appeared from the back door with a white garbage bag and blood sprayed across his shirt.

Tez stood up and dusted his clothes off before picking up his DSK. "What's good, big homie?"

Rayjon looked down at the dead female and nodded his head in approval. "Damn, I love how you niggas get down. Y'all make me miss my li'l brother." He waved us over to him. "Come on, I got the dope. Now let's go next door and get these choppahs so we can get that pay-out."

Chapter 7

I don't know if luck was on our side or what, but as we left through the back of the bar there were two people coming out of the back door of the tattoo parlor. So, as soon as their door opened, Rayjon ain't waste no time bum-rushing they assed wit' me and Tez right behind him on bitness.

Their door was only about ten feet away from the one we came through, so it was an easy attack. Rayjon slammed the butt of his gun right into the first dude's forehead, causing the man to fall backward, then he aimed and busted the other nigga quick. *Boom!* The flash lit up the dark night, illuminating our li'l area. The dude he busted fell backward into the shop, and that's when I rushed in after jumping over his body with my Masburg out, ready for war. Tez was right behind me.

The shop was dimly lit wit' reggaetón playing on some speakers I couldn't locate. As I rushed through the door, I saw a Mexican nigga wit' plenty of tattoos tatting up a real fat dude who was lying on his back, getting ink on his stomach. I didn't know if they were doped up or what, but it seemed like it took them forever to react to our invasion. By the time they did, I had the barrel of my Masburg down the throat of the Mexican nigga who was inking the other stud. I mean I had that muthafucka all the way down there, too. So much so that he was gagging and choking on it.

"Don't move, bitch," I said, thirsty to pull that trigger.

Tez smacked the fat nigga with the butt of his DSK and put the barrel to his forehead before Rayjon came over and grabbed the nigga I had pinned down up by his hair.

T.J. Edwards

"Where them guns at, nigga? And mind you, I'm only gon' ask you once before shit get ugly."

The skinny Mexican looked at him and curled his upper lip. He had spit all over his mouth. It looked nasty as a muthafucka, and his eyes were watery from choking on the barrel of my gun.

"Me speak-a no English, muthafucka," he said, mugging the shit out of Rayjon.

Rayjon turned his head to the side. "Oh, really? That's how you wanna play shit, huh? A'ight." He pointed at me. "Li'l homie, hold this nigga steady for a minute while I lock all of these doors. I'm finna show you how fast all that tough shit disappears when that blade gets introduced to a nigga's ass."

He ran around closing all the windows and locking doors while Tez pressed his gun into the fat Mexican's eye and constantly moved his finger around over the trigger of his weapon. I could tell he was ready to body the dude's ass. The fat nigga was still as hell. I imagined he was beyond spooked.

By the time Rayjon came back, I had the skinny nigga sitting in a chair with the pump to the back of his head. I was hoping whatever Rayjon was getting ready to do wouldn't take him that long. It was already after four in the morning, and I didn't know what morning life in Humboldt Park was like. All I knew was we didn't belong over there, and every minute we wasted in that shop we were playing wit' our lives.

Rayjon pulled his knife out, walked up to the skinny Mexican, and grabbed his throat before slicing the blade across the side of his face real slowly.

"Ah! Fucker! What are you doing to me?" he growled and shook in his chair like he was about to fall out of it.

As the blade traveled across his cheek, a long line of blood appeared. Rayjon trailed the blade across one

Ski Mask Cartel

cheek and all the way to the other side. "Where them guns at, my nigga?" he asked, grabbing him roughly by the throat again.

Now the skinny nigga acted like he wanted to talk. He sat up straight in his seat and everything.

"Downstairs, *vato*. The key is in my pocket, man. It's in the storage. Take them, homes. Just get the fuck out of my store!" he hollered, kicking his legs.

"Gimme the muthafucking key, then. And get yo' punk ass up!" Rayjon said, pulling him out of his seat aggressively.

The skinny Mexican hopped up and went into his pocket, handing Rayjon a keychain of keys. "Look, it's the small silver one. All the guns in the storage locker downstairs, way in back. They're yours, man. I'll take you right to them," he whimpered like a bitch.

"No, the fuck you don't! They'll kill us if you give this motherfucker those guns. What are you thinking?" the fat Mexican hollered from under Tez.

Tez put his forearm to his throat, causing him to gag. He looked like he was trying to get up.

"Big homie, let me smoke this nigga, man. Come on, Jo," he pleaded.

Rayjon waved him off. "Fuck that nigga. Body him, kid. Word is bond."

Tez straightened his back, pressed the gun into the fat Mexican's eye, and pulled the trigger. *Boom! Boom! Boom!* The back of his head exploded and coated the floor with his plasma and brain matter.

The skinny Mexican dropped to his knees and started to shake. "Holy fuck, man. Why would you do that?" he cried.

I was feeling some type of way because there I was thinking all of them Mexican dudes out west got down and was cold hearted, when this skinny nigga was acting like a straight bitch. And I ain't talking female. I mean our hood version of a bitch, meaning soft, weak, a wimp, and so on and so forth. I was embarrassed for the nigga.

Rayjon snatched him up and took him downstairs, and I followed close behind until we got to the storage area he was talking about. It was all wooden and looked like a big-ass wooden box with a padlock hanging on the front of it.

"Grab this nigga, kid, and let me see if this key work."

I wrapped my arm around the skinny nigga's neck and pressed my Masburg under his chin. I was hoping he didn't move because even though it wouldn't have bothered me to kill him, I just didn't want his brain splashing all over me. Not only did that shit stank, but I didn't know if this nigga had a disease or something, so I had visions of killing him while he stood a distance from me.

He shook under me. "I swear they're all there. Please don't kill me, man. I got two daughters and a new wife that just came over from Mexico. All I wanna do is my tats, man. That's it."

I jerked him back to me. "Man, shut yo' bitch ass up. I ain't trying to hear all that muthafuckin' whining. Take this shit like a man and have some dignity for yo' daughters. Right now, you acting like a real bitch."

He started to shake harder.

Rayjon popped the lock and pulled the door open to the storage container, and lo and behold, there the guns were in metal crates. All the tops of the crates were open, so we could easily make out the weaponry.

"Kill that nigga, kid," Rayjon said, pulling one of the crates out into the basement before picking up an AR-33 assault rifle. He turned it over in his hands and nodded his head. "Yeah, smoke that nigga. Hurry up."

Ski Mask Cartel

The skinny nigga jerked his head backward and slammed it into my vest, then tried to get up and run toward the stairs, but that Masburg handled bitness. *Boom! Boom!* The bullets slammed into his back and left two big-ass holes, knocking him forward.

He fell against the steps and bled out before Tez came down them and kicked him to the side.

***

Later the next afternoon, after I had gotten about three hours of sleep, I woke up with a text from the mother of the little girl who had gotten shot a few weeks back. She asked me if I was available to meet up with her, and even though I didn't know what she wanted to meet up for, I met her at 52nd and Aberdeen, which was right in the heart of Moe Town in Chicago.

Moe Town was home of the famous Black P. Stones. They were a crazy black mob known for killing their victims by blowing their heads clean off their necks. Most of the niggas rocked long cornrows or dreads that fell down their backs. I didn't really have a problem wit' any of them, but I still made sure I had my vest strapped on tight and double-breasted with two .45s.

When Jill answered the door, she had a little girl standing on the side of her. She looked to be about Madison's age, very pretty, and a little slim. Jill moved her out of the way and opened the screen door to her crib.

"Little girl, go to your room and clean it up. Get out of my face for a while. I'm not gon' tell you again." The little girl ran off, and Jill looked up at me and smiled.

Even though the sun was shining, the snow was still coming down with the wind blowing like crazy. Nobody had shoveled her porch or her walkway, so it was a task just getting to her front door.

T.J. Edwards

I still didn't know why I ultimately came that day. I guess I was just trying to imagine how I would feel if something ever happened to Madison. I'd need as much support as I possibly could get in order to hang on. Then I factored in she was female and a mother, so it had to be hard for her. I didn't think there was any dude in the picture at the time, but I wasn't sure.

She smiled and opened the door further. "I'm surprised you actually came, Racine. I was expecting you to put me off or somethin'."

I could smell Febreze coming from her house. It smelled good and a little refreshing. "I'm 'bout to put you off if you don't invite me in. It's cold as hell out here, and you already know these Stone niggaz don't play no games. So, what's good?"

She grabbed my arm and pulled me inside. "Damn, what you think I was opening the door all the way for?" She closed the door behind us and I stomped my boots off on her mat before taking them off altogether.

Looking around, her crib was basic. A couch in the living room, a glass table with some ornaments. She already had her Christmas tree up, though there weren't any presents underneath it. She had sheets on her windows acting as curtains, and the front room had a big screen television in it, along with a three-piece furniture set. The white carpet was a little gray, but all in all her place was straight. I could tell she was a female who tried her best to keep things together.

I saw her daughter's obituary hanging on the wall over the window, and it gave me a heavy heart.

After ten minutes of chopping it up, she finally got around to why she really called me over there. "Racine, first, I wanna thank you for paying for my little girl's funeral. If it wasn't for you, I didn't know how I was going to pay for it all, so I thank you for that."

72

She took a deep breath, and I could tell something was wrong wit' her. She was sitting across from me on the couch while I sat in a love seat. Her face looked like she was going through a bunch of emotions. I thought about trying to press her forward, so she would tell me what was on her mind, but I decided to let her speak in her own time.

She took another deep breath and lowered her head. "I know who killed my baby, and I don't know what to do about it." She was quiet for a short while. "This hood got a 'no snitching' policy in place, so if I say anything to the police, they gon' kill me and my daughter, and I don't want that. But I'm so scared. Even though I wanna say something, I'm not going to. But I feel like since they know I know, they are going to kill me and her anyway. I need to get out of this hood, and fast. I hate Chicago," she spat, then placed her hands over her face and began to sob.

I slid from my couch to hers and wrapped my arms around her. She adjusted so her face was lying against my chest. Her crying intensified. I really didn't know what to say to her, and I must've swallowed a hundred times. "Jill. Just. That's messed up, but if there's any way I can help you, I will. All you gotta do is let me know what's good." I tried to pick her face up, so I could look into her eyes, but she kept it buried into my chest.

I started to rock with her just a little bit, holding her close. "Look, if you want, you and your daughter can grab y'all stuff right now and we can bounce up outta here. I'll help you find a crib somewhere else. You ain't gotta go through this bull crap, shorty. That's my word."

She raised her head and looked me in the face with her cheeks covered in tears. She shook her head. "I ain't got no money, Racine. I'm hurting, and the little money I do get barely is enough to pay my rent here. My daughter constantly growing out of her clothes and shoes. The state keep cutting my assistance. Ain't nobody helping me do nothing, and it is hard in these streets for a single woman with a daughter." Snot appeared on her upper lip before she sniffed it back into her nostrils. "I don't know what to do, honestly."

I felt horrible for her, and I got to imagining something bad happening to me, and Kenosha being in the world all on her own with nobody to help her. I would hope some stand-up man would step in and do what's right by her, just due to the fact she was a fighting black woman. I can't understand why more men didn't go hard for our women the way they were supposed to.

"Look, Jill, I got you. What we'll do is put you up in a hotel for a few weeks. I'll foot the bill, and while you're there we'll try and find you another crib on the other side of town. I don't want you worrying about nothing. I got you."

That same night I told Kenosha what the deal was wit' her, and I guess her situation got the better of her heart as well, because instead of me putting Jill up into a hotel, she wound up moving into the guest bedroom of the house I'd just bought Kenosha. It turned out the two girls knew each other and had gone to Fenger High School together. I thought that was cool. I still told Jill I would help her find a crib as soon as possible, and I would fit the bills until she got on her feet.

Two nights later, as she was settling into her room and Madison and Jill's daughter Remy were off in Madison's room playing, I sat her down and grabbed her hands, looking her in the eyes. "Look, I know you used to being independent and on your own, but what you doing right now is smart. I mean, you say you grew up in that hood, so you know them niggas by heart. You felt like they were gon' do something to you and your kid, and you found a way to protect her. I honor you for that. Here," I said, handing her fifteen hundred dollars.

Ski Mask Cartel

She took the money with her eyes wide open. I could tell she was caught off guard. "No, you've already done enough. You don't have to do this," she started.

I pushed her hand away politely as she tried to hand the money back to me. "Look, that ain't nothin' but pocket change. You gon' need that just to feel a li'l human while you trying to get back on yo' feet. When you spend all of that, just let me know and I'll hit you again. I want you to feel like a strong woman and not a dependent. Like I told you before, I got you. Just believe in that, okay?"

She hopped off the bed and wrapped her arms around my neck, crying. "Ain't nobody ever did nothing for me in my life. I've been hurt so much and been screwed over by so many people." She paused and sniffed loudly. "I can't believe that you're doing all of this for me. I swear I'm gon' pay you back. I swear with everything I am as a woman."

In my opinion, she didn't owe me a thing. I felt like she needed somebody to hold her down, and why shouldn't it have been me? I felt like every woman needed a real man to stand up and protect them from this cold world. It wasn't just her in need of protection, but it was her daughter as well. I felt like I was obligated to step in, and I really didn't care what nobody thought about it.

Ironically, Jill got the call that her house was shot up that night and had more than 300 slugs popped into it before it was set on fire and burned to the ground.

My mother always said God worked in mysterious ways. Well, had I not gone over there and got with her, I felt like her and her daughter would have been murdered.

T.J. Edwards

Chapter 8

Rayjon introduced me and Tez to his badass fiancée three days later at the birthday party he threw for her at Vinceno's, which was an upscale night club. Her name was Averie, and when I first saw her – I ain't even gon' lie – her presence had my heart beating fast as a muthafucka. She was about five feet, five inches tall, 130 pounds, brown eyes, short curly hair, and so thick I couldn't take my eyes off the red-and-black Prada mini-dress that was painted onto her frame. Her body was cool as hell, and to top it all off, she was slightly bowlegged.

There were about twenty people there, and I had chosen to bring Kenosha along with me, although I usually wasn't in the business of letting her meet the niggas I did dirt with outside of Tez. But since Tez let Raven come, I felt it was alright. That way they could keep each other company.

Rayjon walked over to me with his arm around Averie as the waiter filled my glass with strawberry Moet. He was fitted in a Prada suit, and I was looking all spiffy in a nice black-and-gray Marc Jacobs fit with the matching number three Jordans. Before I left the house that morning, I noted my waves were popping. Tez was cool wit' cutting hair, so he gave me a quick lining and I was good to go. Even though I was in the streets on that grimy shit, I always made it my business to keep myself up. Most of the niggas I knew in the slums that was in the life seemed to think it was cool to wear the same clothes every single day just because they considered themselves to be grinding. Well, not me. Every day I had to shower and make sure my goatee was lined up nice. On top of that, I had a thing for dressing

T.J. Edwards

nice and smelling good, so I wasn't your average stick-up kid.

Rayjon walked in front of me and stopped, taking his arm from around Averie. "Yo, Racine. This my lady right here. Shorty been down wit' a nigga since day one. I done told her a lot about you, and she wanted to meet you face-to-face. So, Averie, Racine. Racine, Averie."

I made eye contact wit' her and felt some type of way almost immediately. She gave me one of them looks that said she'd eat me alive, but I'd enjoy every second of her chewing on me. I extended my hand to shake hers. I knew that was kinda corny, but I didn't know what else to do.

She frowned for a brief second before nudging my hand to the side and stepping in front of me, wrapping her arms around my body to hug her close. "We don't do that hand shaking shit here, baby. If Rayjon invited you to my birthday party, then that means he look at you like family, so I do, too."

I felt her hot breath on the side of my face, then her perfume went up my nose. She felt so soft and inviting. I damn near didn't want to let her go. I knew I held her way longer than I was supposed to, but Rayjon didn't say shit, so I didn't either. When I released her, we locked eyes again, but this time she looked at the floor as if she felt guilty about somethin'.

Rayjon put his arm back around her possessively. "Yeah, this my baby. I'll kill a muthafucka over her quick. She knows that, too. Ain't that right, li'l lady?"

She slowly nodded her head, then just for a brief second, she raised her eyes to look at me, only to divert them away again. Her eyes had a kind of sadness to them I couldn't really explain. I could just tell somethin' wasn't right.

"Well, anyway, it's nice meeting you, Averie. I really didn't know what to get you for your birthday, so I

78

just got you this li'l diamond tennis bracelet," I said, handing her the rectangular box from Harry Winston's. Her eyes lit up before she grabbed the box and opened it, pulling the bracelet from it and looking it over closely. "Thank you, Racine. This is really nice."

She smiled, stepped forward, and gave me a hug just as Tez walked over with a bottle of Patron in his hand, already open. He looked me up and down, took a swig from the bottle, and wiped his mouth with the same hand he was holding the bottle in. "Damn, nigga, you just a trick. I had to come over here just to make sure you were giving shorty some jewelry. You just met her. You ain't have to give her all of that."

She scrunched her face at him, then looked to Rayjon. "Uh, excuse you, Tez, but you don't know me like that, either. Especially to be speaking up on what he gave me. At least he had enough courtesy to bring me somethin'. It's more than what you thought to do." She rolled her eyes and placed the bracelet back into the box.

Tez looked her up and down before closing his eyes and taking a sip from the Patron. "Shorty, I'm a street nigga. What the fuck I look like, tricking off on a female for period? You ain't in these streets every day risking yo' life to get the chips it'll take to buy that shit he just gave you. This shit is real." He shook his head and turned the bottle back up, swallowing large portions of the liquor.

Averie looked like she wanted to say something, but Rayjon cut in. "Yo, even though you ain't wrong for what you saying, Tez, you gotta watch how you talking to her. This still my woman, so you gotta respect her presence. Far as this gift goes, Racine, I don't know if she gon' be able to keep this." He snatched it out of her hand. "She gotta earn shit like this, and for the last few weeks she been slacking in a few areas. And she know what I'm talking about," he said, looking her in the eyes.

T.J. Edwards

She lowered her head and exhaled loudly.

I put my hand out as he handed me back the box. "My bad, big homie. It took me a whole hour to try to figure out what to bring her. Finally, I asked a few of the ladies in my circle, and this is what they settled on. I ain't mean no disrespect by it."

He put his hand up. "I already know, li'l bruh. But she only get shit like this when I say she should. That's all."

Averie looked sick to her stomach. She made a sour face and took another deep breath. I ain't gon' even lie, the way she was looking all defeated and shit made me want to put my arms around her and tell her it was gon' be okay. I felt like my niggas was ganging up on her, and it was technically still her birthday.

Tez laughed. "You still a better man than me, because I ain't tricking my chips on no female. That's what they got jobs out there for. A muthafucka never call me Captain Save-A-Ho." He put the bottle back to his lips.

Averie slowly shook her head. "May I be excused, Rayjon? I ain't feeling so good," she said without taking her eyes from the floor.

Rayjon nodded. "Yeah, go fuck wit' some bitchez or somethin'. Don't let me catch you in no nigga face or it's gon' be one."

She nodded and began to walk away from us before stopping. "I still think it was a nice gift, Racine. And even though I couldn't keep it, I appreciated it. So, thank you, and enjoy the rest of the party." She turned and walked away.

I ain't gon' even lie, as much as I tried not to, I couldn't help but catch one last glimpse of that booty. I still couldn't believe how perfect it was. I wasn't ridiculous, though, because I figured Rayjon was onto me, so I glanced and kept it moving.

Ski Mask Cartel

"Aw, you ain't gon' say bye to me? That's what we on? A'ight, that's cool. Well, happy birthday to you anyway, Averie," Tez said, slurrin' his words.

She waved him off and kept right on walking until she disappeared into a crowd of females where Kenosha and Raven were.

The music seemed like it got louder all the sudden, and it felt like a few more people had come into the party since I got there. I wasn't sure if that was what happened or not, but it definitely felt like it.

"We got a new contract already. I'm talking seventy-five gees apiece, but this time it's strictly about torturing some niggas on behalf of a client. You niggas up to it?" Rayjon asked, lightin' a blunt.

Seventy-five thousand sounded like good money. I was already spending it in my head. I knew I had to get Jill and her daughter right, then I wanted to put her in some kind of Whip because, at that time, she was riding the bus or getting drove around by me or Kenosha. Even though Kenosha didn't act like she had a problem with it, I felt that over time she probably would have. Then, in regards to Kenosha, I wanted to pay up another six months on her car note and the rent. Then I had to keep on making sure my mother's bills were paid. So, I had a nice li'l plate, not to mention my daughter had to stay in the top-of-the-line, and it was her right to have me provide whatever she wanted or needed. Before I could even think about my own needs, that li'l seventy-five bands was damn near gone.

"Jo, I'm down for whatever gon' keep getting me that paper. I don't give a fuck who we gotta hit up. Let's just handle that bitness so I can get my scratch," Tez said, slurring his words.

"What about you, Racine? You fuckin' wit' this mission?" Rayjon asked, looking Kenosha up and down as she walked over to us with her Gucci bag over her shoulder.

I nodded. "I'm down, bro. Just let me know where and when and what we gotta do."

Rayjon smiled and took a deep pull from his blunt.

Kenosha came over and grabbed my hand. "Racine, I need to talk to you, and I mean right now," she said, sounding a little angry.

"Say, let me see what's good wit' my BM, bro. I'll holler at you niggas in a minute. Just let me know what's good and when we gon' sit down on this bitness."

Rayjon nodded. "Will do, my nigga. Love, fool."

Tez just smiled and shook his head before walking off.

Me and Kenosha wound up sitting in her car with the heat on. It was so cold outside that when she first turned the heat on, it blew out cold air. It took us a little while to get comfortable enough to talk because it was freezing out there.

"Where you know that bitch from, Racine?" she asked out of the blue with a frown on her face. She rubbed her arms, trying to warm herself, looking me over closely.

"Who you talking about, shorty?"

"That bitch whose party it is. Where do you know her from, and why do she think she can come up to me and tell me how fine and nice my baby daddy is? What, you told this bitch we not together or something? And ain't she fucking wit' that skinny nigga that was at the party with the long braids?"

I sat up in the seat as the vents finally started to blow out some form of heat. "Man, you talking about Averie? The li'l thick broad that fuck wit' Rayjon?"

She rolled her eyes and then looked at the ceiling of the car, huffing and puffing like she was losing her temper. "I can't believe this nigga just said that. Yeah, nigga, I'm talking about the li'l thick bitch. Who is this ho? And why you have me help you pick out a gift for her?"

I ran my hand over my face. I really hated arguing or fighting wit' my BM. Honestly, I didn't like getting into it wit' nobody I cared about because my temper was lethal. As long as I had been in Kenosha's life, I had never raised my hand to her, but she was famous for pushing the envelope. "Look, I just met her today. I ain't never said a word to her before then. Far as the gift go, I didn't know what to get a female for her birthday that I didn't know, which is why I asked for you and my mother's opinion. That's it."

"So why is she calling you fine and shit or pulling me to the side and sayin' 'I don't mean no disrespect, but that man you came in with is not only fine, but he's a sweetheart. I wish more niggas was like him.'" She scrunched her face. "I don't wanna hear no bitch talking about you like that. That shit irritates me, and I don't like being jealous over other hos. These bitches ain't have yo' kid. I did."

Every time Kenosha got to feeling some type of way, she always managed to bring up the fact of her having Madison, and it never failed to weaken me a little bit. Due to the fact she had my daughter, in my eyes it meant she deserved the utmost respect. "Look, I don't know why shorty said that shit to you, and I can't control her tongue. However, me and you ain't together on that level. We already established that we were too young to be trying to be all monogamous and shit. You got some things in you that you want to explore, and I do as well. We definitely ain't finna play them type of games."

She lowered her head. "I know what we agreed upon. I just hate when other bitches choose you in my face. It makes me feel sick to the stomach, because when it's all said and done, you promised me, and you were going to be together. I just don't want no female slipping in and taking my slot. I'd rather die than not have you as my husband one day."

I pulled her over to me and kissed her on the forehead. "I don't give a fuck what I'm doing in them streets. I'll never let nobody steal yo' slot. You're my baby, and I got you even after my last breath. You know that." I raised her chin to make her look at me. "Since we been together, have you ever needed or wanted for anything?"

She shook her head. "Nall, never. And that's what I'm afraid of. I'm afraid one day you gon' find some bitch in these streets that's gon' make you forget about how much I mean to you. Then what will I have? Not a damn thing, because the other niggas in this world ain't like you. All they care about is themselves."

She sucked on her bottom lip, then looked out of her window. Snow fell from the sky heavily, landing on the windshield of the car and covering it while we sat there in silence for a few minutes. I didn't know what to say to her. I knew I would never forget about Kenosha. She was embedded too deep within my heart and soul. I didn't know how I could convince her she had nothing to worry about without feeding her a bunch of bullshit lines, and that wasn't my style. Since I had been a part of her life, I had never lied to her, and I never would.

I pulled her over to me and held her close. "Baby, I love you. Can't no other female out there tell you I have ever said those three words to them. But I love you with all my heart. We're just young right now, and we're figuring shit out as we go, but I already know I will never put anybody before you. That shit just ain't happening. You're my heart, and that will never change. Now gimme them lips."

Ski Mask Cartel

She sucked her teeth loudly and looked at me for a brief second before closing her eyes, leaning over, and kissing my lips. I tongued her li'l ass down for a full three minutes before sucking on her neck and biting it. We both started breathing hard, and I could feel my dick getting hard.

"Just keep me first, daddy, and I don't care what you do wit' these hos. Just let them know I'm first."

She moaned as my hand went under her short dress and pulled her panties to the side, exposing that fat kitty before squeezing her sex lips together and sucking her juices off my fingers.

I bit into her neck. "Baby, you my one through seven. I tell you that every single day."

I pulled her short dress up all the way and pulled her onto my lap. She reached between us and freed my dick before sliding backward onto him hard.

"Huh! Shit, daddy! Please let me ride you. I need to cum on my daddy real fast. Please, Racine," she whimpered, bouncing up and down on me like crazy.

I bit into her neck and held her hips, slamming her up and down my pole. Her pussy felt more hot than usual. The way she was gripping me caused me to make a few noises I wasn't proud of.

She bounced faster and faster. "This my dick, daddy. This big-ass dick is mine. I don't want nobody doing this shit like this but me. Ah shit!" she screamed and started to hump me like an animal.

I pulled her shoulder straps down, exposing her B-cup titties and squeezing them together before sucking her big nipples. Kenosha had nipples that resembled baby pacifiers. Them muthafuckas drove me crazy. I even liked the way my BM's breasts sagged just a little bit. They were au natural, and I appreciated that.

She got to bouncing up and down, moaning loudly. "Mm! Daddy! Daddy, I'm cumming. Daddy! I'm cumming all over my daddy! Mm fuck, baby!" she screamed, digging her nails into my shoulders.

I wrapped my arms around her and came deep within her channel while I sucked all over them titties.

Chapter 9

My eyes got bucked as hell as I watched Rayjon rip the fat white man's shirt off him and throw it to the floor like he was pissed off. We were in a bowling alley with the place locked down. I was sweating so bad under my mask that it was itchin' the hell out of me.

Tez finished tying up the last of the three men in chairs and pulled a long knife out of the inside of his fatigue jacket, then walked over to me. "Nigga, you good? I know you used to using that banger and all, but you don't know how good it feels to kill a muthafucka until you kill they ass using a knife. I'm finna enjoy this shit. Bullshit ain't about nothin'." he walked over to another white dude in a business suit and slapped the shit out of him.

I was too busy trying to figure out what the fuck we were doing in a bowling alley wit' three white men tied up, and Rayjon had given the order we were gon' torture they ass to death. I didn't know what was going on, and even though I knew how much money I was gon' get, I still didn't like not being in the know.

Tez acted like he didn't give a fuck. To him, all white men represented was money. I mean, I didn't really have a problem getting down for that paper, but in my mind shit just had to make sense to me. Like I said before, I had too much common sense.

Rayjon walked over to me and pointed at the last white man Tez had tied up. He was a li'l slim with a long black ponytail, though he was balding on the top of his head. "I want you to torture this bitch-nigga while I record this shit for my client. He wanna be able to watch the whole scene back, so I need for you to really fuck 'em up. Then li'l bruh gon' handle that bitch right there. We do this shit right and we ain't gotta worry about no

T.J. Edwards
jobs for a long time because they gon' be supplied to us."

I nodded my head, opened my fatigue jacket, and unleashed the deer hunting knife Rayjon gave me about two hours back. I walked over to the skinny white dude and looked down on him with hatred. I didn't know why he was in the position he was in, but in order for me to do what I had to do, I had to imagine he had hurt one of the females in my family in some sort of way.

"Slice that muthafucka up, cuz. All three of these bitch-ass muthafuckas is judges, and they done screwed over plenty niggas of our pigment just, so they could line they pockets. These muthafuckas ain't shit but slave traders. Punish they bitch ass," Rayjon said, sounding angry.

That was all I needed to hear. I looked down on the man and curled my upper lip under my mask. I got to imagining him selling my pops up the river for a li'l bit of nothing, then laughing about it wit' the other men. Then I imagined how they looked down at men and women of my color when they came before them in a courtroom and I just snapped. I slashed the knife through the air and sliced the man across his face three times while he stomped his feet and screamed into his gag. I ain't feel no sympathy for him.

To my left Tez was going in on his victim, slashing him across the face and neck while Rayjon recorded him. Feeling left out, I got on bitness.

I imagined we were back in the roots days and this white man had touched my mother. I grabbed him by the ponytail and brought my knife across his face repeatedly while his blood spurted into the air and he struggled against his bonds.

Rayjon came over and moved me out of the way. He kicked the man in the chest, causing him to fall

88

backward in his chair. "Alright, kneel down and stab his bitch ass until yo' arm get tired. Really fuck him up."

I did just as he ordered. Raising the knife over my head, I brought it down into the man's chest with all my might. The blade ripped through his skin and put a hole right in his chest. He heaved upward, and I brought it down again while he screamed into his gag and shook his head from right to left, probably begging me to spare his life.

I could only imagine what he was feeling, but I didn't have time to dwell on it. I stabbed him again and again, leaving big gashes in his chest. Then I went down to his stomach and repeated the process, stabbing and stabbing until he quit moving. I stood up and looked down at my work.

Rayjon slapped me on the back. "Job well muthafucking done, my nigga. That's what I'm talking about," he said, then took the phone and slowly walked over to where Tez was handling his bitness on the fat white man. Rayjon recorded him, nodding his head.

Tez grabbed the white man by the throat roughly and stabbed him in the stomach repeatedly, while the man screamed into his duct tape, then his head fell backward with his eyes wide open, looking at the ceiling, yet it didn't stop my cousin from stabbing him again and again until he got tired. Only then did he step back and kick the man in the chest. He fell backward in the chair, before it landed on its side with him still duct-taped to it. "Bitch-ass crackers. That shit felt so good."

Rayjon handed me the phone. "Look, li'l homie, make sure you catch everything I'm finna do to this muthafucka right here, because this the main one my client wants fucked over. A'ight?" he said, walking over to the judge after picking up a red and black marble bowling ball.

T.J. Edwards

"Yeah, I got you, big homie," I said, watching Tez walk behind him.

Rayjon walked over to the judge and kicked him in the chest just like he'd did the one I'd killed. The man fell backward in the chair. "Li'l homie, hold dude's head while I bash his shit in wit' this bowling ball."

"Now that's what the fuck I'm talking about," Tez said, sounding excited. He knelt down and grabbed the man by the head. He had one hand on each side of the man's face, holding it tight.

I could hear the man screaming into the duct tape. I didn't know what the fuck he was saying. I figured he was begging for his life, but it was too late.

Rayjon raised the bowling ball wit' one hand and mugged the shit out of the judge. "Rest in hell, you racist muthafucka!" He brought the ball down at full speed. It crashed into the man's face and caved it in. He raised it again and slammed it down, this time so hard blood spurted out of the man's ears. The man's body started to shake real bad, and that made Tez start laughing.

I was starting to think I was around two sick-ass niggas, because they both looked like they were taking pleasure in killin' these dudes where, in my mind, it was all for the paper. I was already imagining how this shit was gon' come back on me through the act of karma. I knew whatever went around came around, and I was gon' die a bloody death. My whole thing was I hoped before I went my daughter and Kenosha had everything they could ever need and want in life. It was the reason I grinded so hard.

"Say, li'l homie, make sure you zoom in on this one right here because this the one that's gon' get that check wrote," he growled, then raised the ball all the way over his head with two hands, then brought it down at full speed, smashing the judge's face inward. More blood oozed out of his ears. When Rayjon stood up, I could

90

see the judge's face looked like it had been hollowed out. From the neck up was a bloody mess.

Tez came over, looked down on him, and started laughing like he was watching a comedy show.

***

The next day I bought me a small safe and stacked my paper up in it. I had a little over $120,000, and I felt I needed at least another 200 gees before I would be able to feel like I was making progress. I was trying to calculate everything in my mind, and every time I thought I had it all figured out, a new bill arose.

That night while Kenosha and Madison were off visiting with my mother, I decided to stay in the crib and just chill for a minute. The Cleveland Cavaliers game was coming on, and since I was a crazy LeBron James fan, I was gon' sit back and watch it while I ate my gyro and chili-cheese fries that I'd brought from John Red Hotts.

The game was in the second quarter and I pulled my sandwich out of the microwave when I felt a hand rubbing on my back. I damn near jumped out of my skin, 'til I saw it was Jill.

"Damn, boy, calm down. It's only me," she said, laughing with her chubby jaws. "I smelled that gyro and it woke me up."

I smiled. "Shorty, you can't be walking up on me like that. You gotta do a better job of announcing yo' self. You already know the life I live," I said, putting my sandwich on a plate and grabbing a knife out of the drawer.

"I know. I know, and that's my bad. Damn, I ain't mean to cause no trouble," she said, putting her hands up. She had on some real pink booty shorts that exposed all her chocolate thighs. Her white tank top was tight around her breasts and exposed the bulge of her stomach through the material.

"You good. I'll cut you half of this sandwich, too, unless you want me to brave the elements and run out and get one. It wouldn't take me that long. Besides, what's good wit' Remy? Is she hungry?" I was trying to remember the last time I had seen the little girl eat something and couldn't remember. I was prepared to go out into the snow to go snatch them up something to put on their stomachs. I didn't feel right feeding my face, not knowing if they had eaten or not.

Jill smiled. "Damn, you got a good heart. Yo' momma gotta be proud of you because you are always thinking about other people."

I was thinking if she only knew what I had done just a few hours back to that judge, she wouldn't be saying nothin' like that.

"But she's in there 'sleep. When she wakes up, I'll make her some ravioli. That's all she like right now. She real picky. But as far as I go, you can share some of yo' sandwich wit' me, if that's cool."

That's just what I did. I gave her more than half of my gyro, and chili-cheese fries. We sat in front of the big screen and watched the game in silence. It turned out she liked LeBron, too, and that was super cool to me because Kenosha wasn't into sports like that.

"He gon' be coming to the city in two weeks, and I want you to go to the game wit' me. I feel like it's time for you to get out of this house and just let yo' hair down. Don't worry about nothin', I'll take care of everything." I put a forkful of food into my mouth and started chewing.

Jill sat her plate on the table in front of us, turned my way, and kissed me on the cheek once real soft, then nuzzled her face into my neck before sucking on it. "I ain't never had no man like you in my life before. You

drive me absolutely crazy, and I'll do anything for you."
She sucked on my neck loudly, then ran her hand across
my chest.

I felt her caresses, and I ain't gon' even lie and say
it didn't feel good, because it did. I swallowed my food
as she straddled my lap and looked down on me. It had
been a while since any female other than Kenosha had
straddled me like that, so the first thing I noted was the
weight difference. Jill was a li'l heavier, but that wasn't
a problem because I was real muscular. So, when she
got up there, the first thing I did was look up at her and
grip that big ass, rubbing it and everything.

"Racine, I don't mean no disrespect to Kenosha or
nothin' like that, but I want you so bad. Like, I need you
in my body. You been doing all this stuff for me, and I
ain't got no way of paying you back. I just want to
please you one time. I'll do anything you want, just tell
me what you need from me." She adjusted herself in my
lap, leaned down, and licked my neck before biting into
it again.

That shit sent chills down my spine, and my dick
was already rock hard and growing. She must've felt it
because she reached between us and grabbed it, moaning into my neck.

As much as I wanted to tear that ass up, I had to keep
at the forefront of my brain that she was in a very vulnerable state of mind at that moment. Not only that, but
she felt indebted to me, and I didn't feel like she was.
And if all those things weren't enough, we were in the
living room of the house that I'd got for Kenosha. That
would have been low as hell of me to get down like that,
and even though me and my BM wasn't technically together in the regular sense of the word, I still respected
her one hunnit percent.

So, I grabbed Jill's hands and held them, looking up
at her. She took her face from my neck and gave me a

confused look. "Jill, I don't like you thinking you owe me somethin' because you don't. You ain't gotta do nothin' you don't want to. I mean that."

She shook her head. "I know that, Racine, but I'm feeling you on that level, and I want to give myself to you because I need you." She blinked, and tears came rolling down her cheeks. "My whole life ain't no man ever gave two fucks about me, and then all of the sudden you come out of the blue and you save me from my situation. Don't you understand I could have been dead if it weren't for you? Me and my daughter."

I looked up at her and wiped her tears from her cheeks. I could still feel her weight on my lap, and that was making my dick jump. I couldn't help that, but I was trying my best to not look at her in a sexual light because I honestly felt in that moment she needed more than that. She needed a real nigga.

I pulled her down and kissed her on the lips, then helped her off my lap and to the side of me, brushing her hair out of her face.

She lowered her head before laying it on my chest. "I'm so confused right now."

I felt sorry for her and like I needed to protect her. I could only imagine what she was going through mentally. "Look, Jill, just on some real shit, if you want me to handle my bitness with this sexy-ass body of yours, I ain't got no problem doing that because I'm definitely feeling you on that level. It's just we couldn't do nothin' like that in my BM's crib. That would be bogus as hell."

She turned to her side and looked at me wit' her eyes bright, rubbing my stomach muscles and squeezing my chest. "I swear to God, I want you to do me in, Racine. I been hearing how you be having Kenosha in there screaming, and I know you know what you doing. Plus, you working wit' a lot. Look at all of this," she said, grabbing my piece through my Ferragamo pants. "We

Ski Mask Cartel

ain't gotta do nothin' in this house, but when we go to the game, you gotta hit this pussy for me. Don't think us big girls don't get down, because we do. I'ma prove that to you. All you gotta do is give me a chance." She squeezed my dick and kissed my cheek.

"Man, long as you getting down because you want to and not because you think you owe me somethin', then we gon' do our thing. Besides, that big girl shit don't mean nothin'. You bad, shorty. Especially after having two kids. You need to take time out to celebrate you, on some real shit." I grabbed her to me and hugged her before making her stand in front of me while I sat down. I took my hands and gripped that ass while she spread her thick legs.

She pulled her shirt up over her stomach. "You mean to tell me this ain't too much for you? That you don't find this gross or nothin'?" She looked me in the eyes, and I could tell her confidence was wavering.

Even though I had never been wit' a big girl before, seeing her stomach didn't turn me off at all. The fact she was a mother and had brought children into the world was enough to make me appreciate her stomach. It had a few stretch marks across it and hung a little over her waistband, but honestly, she was still very sexy to me, and it didn't take away from her sex appeal one bit.

I leaned forward and kissed all over it, then pulled her back down to my lap. "You good, shorty. I'ma prove all of that to you, though. You'll see."

She looked at me for a long time before smiling and rubbing the sides of my face. "You gon' make me fall in love wit' yo' ass, then Kenosha gon' kill me because I already know she ain't coming up off you like that. And you the type of nigga I'd be willing to die over."

T.J. Edwards

Chapter 10

Shit got real crazy three days later, and I still can't believe how me and Tez was blindsided. We pulled into the gas station on 104th and Cottage Grove just as it was starting to rain real bad. The homie Twista was having an after party out in Harvey, Illinois, which is basically another suburb of Chicago, and me and Tez had our minds set on making an appearance because it was supposed to be cracking. Neither one of us really knew Twista like that, but being from Chicago, he was like our own personal rapper for the city, next to Kanye.

Tez was in his truck, already fucked up off two pills of X and a quarter bottle of Patron. He was so screwed he couldn't drive, so I found myself behind the wheel playing the designated driver. We had three li'l hood rats in the car that he knew, and I didn't, and they were headed to the same destination. I didn't know what they were going to do when they got there, but I definitely wasn't fuckin' wit' them on that level, although I figured Tez was.

As I pulled into the BP gas station, it started raining hard as hell and Tez's oil light popped on. "Say, cuz, when was the last time you put some oil in this muthafucka?" I asked, pulling beside a gas pump and throwing the truck in park.

He leaned forward and squinted his eyes at the dashboard, I guessed to see the oil light better. I could tell he was fucked up because he looked like he was having a tough time holdin' his head up. "I can't remember, Jo. But if that muthafucka light popped on, that mean it been a while. Snatch some o' that shit up when you go in there and pay for the gas."

I snapped my neck to mug that nigga. "Yo, why am I paying for yo' gas and yo' oil, nigga? I already gotta

drive yo' crazy ass around like you Ms. Daisy or somethin'. Ain't nobody tell ya ass to get fucked up this early,
cuz. Fo' real, I ain't about to be yo' butler and shit."

One of the dark-skinned hood rats in the back of the
truck spoke up. I didn't know her name. "Damn, Jo, you
ain't gotta come at the homie like that. If it's that big of
a problem, I'll pay fo' the gas and the oil. Small thangs
to a boss bitch. Am I right, Tez?" she said, leaning all
over his seat.

Tez looked over his shoulder and nodded. "Yeah,
shorty, that's what I'm talking about. Get yo' ass out
and go pay for everything, then have one of yo' home-
girls pump my shit. Regular fo' gas and 5W30 synthetic
oil. I'll put the oil in it myself. You hos probably don't
know how to do that." He laughed and sparked a blunt.

She rolled her eyes and looked over her shoulder.
"Kee-Kee, you pump the gas and I'll go pay for this shit.
Let's hurry up 'cuz you already know how Tez get when
he get irritated."

She opened the side door and her and a light-skinned
female I guessed was Kee-Kee got out. I didn't really
see what they looked like physically from the waist up
until they walked in front of the truck and headed into
the gas station. It was only then I saw they were both
strapped with big-ass booties. Now I was thinking about
getting to know they asses a li'l better.

"Tez, you know you can holler at us better than that,
too. Damn, you ain't got no respect for females," the
brown-skinned sista in the back seat said, texting somebody on her cellphone. She didn't even bother to look
up from it as she chastised Tez.

Tez shrugged his shoulders. "All you hos already
know how I get down, and y'all keep fuckin' wit' me
anyway. And it ain't that I ain't got no respect for you
bitches, it's just I am how I am. Y'all can respect that or

kiss my hairy ass." He took another swallow from the Patron and laughed.

"Well, I ain't gon' do neither one. The only reason I'm here is because my sister like yo' crazy ass and I wanna make sure she's safe when she wit' you. That's the only reason, trust me."

Tez scrunched his face, looked at me for a brief second, then turning around to face her. "Bitch, we all just had a threesome together two days ago. Was you just there to make sure that she was safe when you were deep-throating a nigga and forcin' my dick up yo' li'l pussy?"

She rolled her eyes and waved him off. "Nigga, that was them pills. I can't be held responsible for what I did the other night." She sat back in her seat and shook her head before getting out of the car, still texting on her phone.

"Bitches be wilding out, cuz, fo' real. I ain't got time to be catering to these hos. I'm just trying to fuck and get some paper. That's it, that's all." He took a strong pull from the blunt and tried to pass it to me, but I moved his hand out of my face.

"I'm good, boss, I'm trying to keep my head. I already know it's finna be plenty niggas here from Chicago, and I wanna make sure we don't miss no enemies' faces. That's why I can't understand why you already fucked up and shit. Damn, nigga." I was a little irritated because that nigga Tez had plenty drama all over Chicago wit' all kinds of niggas. I didn't think I was gon' be able to catch every nigga we were into it wit', plus the other hundred he'd kicked some shit off wit' when we weren't together. I was starting to not even wanna go to the party altogether.

Tez burped and blew it out, hitting himself on the chest. "Fuck all them niggas, Jo. If it come down to it, then we'll just have to let our guns bark. I never get tired of killing these bitch-ass niggas anyway. I love this shit," he said, smiling.

Kee-Kee knocked on the window and I rolled it down. "Pop the gas cap so I can pump this shit." She walked to the back of the truck and I flipped the switch. "That's how you gotta have these hos, cuz. These bitches supposed to work for us. It's been like that since the beginning of time," Tez said, pulling off the blunt.

I shook my head. "Nigga, yo' lazy ass could have pumped that gas. I know you betta get out and put that oil in that shorty walking over here wit' or this mutha-fucka finna burn up," I said, watching the gas station fill up with more cars.

Tez put his blunt into the ashtray and sat the bottle of Patron on his seat before opening the passenger's door. I watched him walk up to the dark-skinned female and grab the bottle of Pennzoil from her before they disappeared behind the hood after I popped it.

Kee-Kee finished pumping the gas and got back into the truck, rubbin' her hands together. "Ugh, I hate the smell of gas. Y'all know it's a man's job to be doing shit like that," she said, making eye contact with me in the rearview mirror.

I smiled. "I would've did it, shorty, but y'all seemed like y'all already had an entire system worked out. That's my bad, though, 'cuz you right." Honestly, I felt like she was. Me and that nigga Tez could've handled that bitness wit' no problem. I felt like a bogus-ass nigga for letting them ladies do that. My mom raised me better than that.

Kee-Kee smiled. "On some real shit though, homie, you fine as hell. I'm feeling them dimples on yo' cheeks, and I love a nigga wit' deep waves. Me and my cousin was just talking about you when we went into the gas station. If it's any fucking going down tonight, I'm trying to dip off wit' you. Straight up." She licked her juicy lips. "You got a problem wit' that?"

I couldn't help but laugh as I looked back there at her thick ass. Facially she was nice, and her body was cole. She looked a li'l young, though. "How old is you, li'l momma?"

She raised an eyebrow. "Really? You probably the first nigga in Chicago to ever ask me that because these niggas don't be caring. But I'm nineteen wit' my own crib and two jobs. What's good?" She crossed her thick thighs and sat back in the seat, causing her skirt to rise. "I'ma promise you this shit good, and if it ain't, nigga, I'll pay you. That's my word."

I watched her raise her skirt and open her legs, revealing purple-laced panties that looked stuffed with kat. I had to turn all the way around in the seat just to see what was good.

Thankfully I did, because as I was looking between shorty's legs I was able to look out the back window just in time to see three cars turn into the gas station at full speed with their tires screeching. Before I could even put two and two together, all three of them stormed into the gas station and slammed on their brakes right on the side on Tez's truck. About five niggas jumped out with handguns and ran up to the truck. One of them slammed his gun into the passenger's window where Tez had been sitting, shattering it before sticking his gun through it. Kee-Kee started to scream at the top of her lungs.

"Bitch-ass nigga, get the fuck out of the truck and break yo' self, fool!" he hollered through the black ski mask.

I could see three of the niggas already outside stripping Tez. I was mad as a muthafucka because I was that nigga that laid kats down. I didn't let that shit happen to me, yet here I was. I took a deep breath and mugged the nigga wit' so much hatred he had to feel it. I didn't move, though.

"Nigga, I'ma tell you one last time. Get the fuck out of the truck and break yo' self."

The driver's side door flew open and another one of the masked niggas yanked me out of the car and threw me to the concrete before stomping me on my back so hard I felt my toes go numb. Then another nigga came over and they started stripping me out of my clothes while Kee-Kee continued to scream and holler inside of the truck before she was thrown down right next to me, crying.

One of the niggas started to strip her out of her clothes, and I felt that shit was unnecessary. One of them had already went all under her skirt doing way too much. They had to know she ain't have shit else on her, but it didn't stop her from being stripped ass-naked just like the rest of us.

As the nigga was taking me out of my clothes, I felt like I was being raped. He was stripping me out of them all rough and everything. By the time he had me down to my boxers, I wanted to kill his bitch ass ten times more.

Finally, after he stripped my boxers off, they threw all that shit into Tez's truck, jumped in, and stormed off.

Me and Tez jumped up at the same time, looking like we wanted to chase the truck, but then figured it would be pointless. I was sick. I didn't even give a fuck I was standing there ass-naked. I was sick because we got caught slipping, and that never happened. We already knew how it was in Chicago. There was an unspoken rule you never took more than five minutes to pump yo' gas unless you were in your own hood, but if you wasn't, then there was a ninety percent chance yo' ass was finna be jacked or murdered, and most times both. So, I felt like we lucked out, to say the least.

Ski Mask Cartel

The females ran into the gas station and said they were going to call the police, and I ran over to a money-green Escalade that pulled into the gas station. The driver was a female and on her way to getting out of the truck when she saw me and rolled down her window. "You a'ight, li'l daddy?"

I shook my head. "Look, some niggas just caught me and my cousin slipping and jacked us. I ain't got no paper on me right now, but if you drop me off at my crib I'll give you a few hunnit for the lift. I stay out in Riverdale."

I heard the locks pop. "You ain't gotta give me shit, baby. Y'all get in and I'll take you there."

I called Tez to the truck and she did just what she said she was gon' do. When we got to my crib I told her to hold on while I ran inside and got her a couple hunnit dollars, but when I got back outside she was gone. I never found out her name or where she was from or none of that, but I always hoped I ran into her again. I just wanted to bless her.

***

Shit got a li'l uneasy when Rayjon introduced two new niggas to the cartel named Wood and Vaughn. He said they were from New Jersey and were 'bout that action just like we was. Out of the gate I already knew me and Tez wasn't gon' get along with these niggas because they were cocky and arrogant.

Rayjon had all four of us over to his crib where his lady, Averie, cooked us dinner consisting of ox tails, brown rice, curry, and a banana pudding pie. She threw down, and I was thankful for the meal. Due to the fact we were supposed to be getting to know each other, Rayjon had her set the dinner table up in the basement

T.J. Edwards

part of their house, and it didn't take none of us that long to start eating.

"Racine, Tez, I want y'all to get familiar wit' my li'l niggas because they gon' help us get rich. It's plenty money out here to get, and the bigger the mob, the bigger the move we'll be able to pull. I used to get down wit' these li'l niggas before I came out here, and I'm telling you they get down for that green," he said, spooning up his brown rice.

Tez grunted. "Mo' niggaz mean mo' ways we gotta split this paper. That shit don't sound like good news to me. Sound like my portion about to be cut in half." He sat sucking on an ox tail.

I knew it wasn't gon' take Tez long to speak his mind. I wanted to know what Rayjon's response was gon' be to that.

Vaughn, a short, stocky nigga wit' glasses, nodded his head before curling his upper lip. "Word is bond, my nigga. We been getting gwop wit' the homie, and our portions ain't never been short, so trust and believe ain't shit like that about to jump off. Secondly, me and my brother don't move unless we taking home a hunnit bands apiece. That's how it's always been."

Wood, a short, dark-skinned nigga wit' a bald head, drank from his fruit punch, swallowed, and put the glass back down. "We from out east, kid. The numbers out there are crazy. I don't know what the fuck go on out here in Chicago, but I know homie would have never had us relocate unless he was finna put us up on paper."

Rayjon stood up. "Yo, I know it's gon' be hard for you niggas to get along at first, but y'all gon' get through that shit then we get this money together. I got love for all four of y'all, and I'm the chief of this cartel, so if I say we all working together, then that's what we gon' do." He wiped his mouth, turned around, and grabbed something rolled up that looked like a poster.

Ski Mask Cartel

He knelt down and unrolled the poster. We all scooted away from the table, dropping our utensils on our plates, and knelt down next to him. "Hold this muthafucka right here, Wood," he said, pointing to the bottom portion of the poster. Then he unrolled it all the way and a picture of the inside of a bank's lobby came into view.

Before he even got to explaining anything, I felt my heart skip a beat because I knew where things were about to go, and I wasn't sure if I was wit' it. I was cool wit' laying niggas down because they couldn't call the police, but robbing a bank was somethin' else because it tripled our chances of going to the feds, and not many niggas got away wit' robbing banks.

"This move right here gon' ensure we make a hunnit thousand dollars apiece. I can guarantee you niggas that."

Vaughn ran his hand across the picture and smiled. "We just hit one about this size a few months ago, big homie, and that shit wasn't that bad. You got muthafuckas in place for this one, too?"

I felt like I had to piss bad as hell all the sudden. Well, I had to piss before I came down to the basement but crouching down like that really had me having to go.

Rayjon nodded. "You already know. See, Racine, what you and Tez don't understand is every time we pulled a move, it was to open a door for another, bigger one. Everything I do is about that paper, large sums, and that's what this cartel is all about. That's how my pops ran his cartel, and that's how I'm gon' run this one."

Tez shrugged his shoulders. "So, when you trying to do this? And what all we need to know about this move? Are we killing everybody, or is it strictly about the paper? I mean, either way is cool wit' me. I'm just trying to get a picture in my head."

"We in it strictly for the paper, and if we can leave this job without killing nobody, then that'd be ideal.

105

However, shit happens," Rayjon said, looking us all over closely.

Wood made a cheesy face, showcasing all his teeth. "I love when shit just happens, though. Word is bond. Ain't nothin' like splashin' a muthafucka over that paper, especially white people."

Vaughn smiled. "I second that motion."

Rayjon looked irritated. "It ain't always good to kill, though, especially when it comes down to moves like this because it make the feds do they jobs ten times harder. So, if we can go in there and handle this business without killing nobody, then that will be ideal. I got a few plugs in place to make sure shit go the way it's supposed to, and over the next few weeks we gon' go over camera surveillance and everything so we can all get a good understanding as to the ins and outs of this bank. We hit this one right and the next job we'll be getting two hunnit apiece. That's not factoring in the other jobs I got lined up for this family. But, in order for us to function as one unit, that's just what we have to function as – one family." He looked from one man to the next before going on.

I had to piss and excused myself. When I got upstairs, I could hear the sounds of SZA coming from the speakers, singing about the weekend. Kenosha played that song so much it gave me a headache. I made my way down the hall and to the bathroom, but when I got to the door it was just opening to reveal Averie with a pink Burberry bath towel wrapped around her.

When she saw me she jumped, and the towel fell from her body, exposing her nudity. I think it caught both of us off guard because even though she yelped, she saw it was me and it seemed like it took her a few seconds to cover her breasts, even though it was a poor attempt because they were a little too big to be covered with one hand. So, she put up two and left her bald pussy exposed. When my eyes looked down and saw how thick her lips were, I got hard immediately.

She bucked her eyes, then knelt down and picked up her bath towel. That finally snapped me out of my zone. "Damn, my bad, Averie. I ain't know you was in there." I felt my man jumping, and I was hoping she didn't see that shit because I was already embarrassed.

She stood up and tightened the towel around her. "It's okay, as long as it's just you. I thought it was one of them other niggas." She smiled and looked me up and down. "You liked what you saw?"

I had to shake my head to make sure I wasn't hearing shit. "What you just say?" I asked, looking into her pretty brown eyes. She smelled so good, fresh out of the shower and all. I had to piss so bad, and that was making my dick swell up even more.

She sucked her bottom lip, stepped forward, and grabbed my dick. "I asked you if you liked what you saw. I mean, you can't un-see what you seen, and it's been so long since another man seen me naked, so I just wanna know if you liked what you saw. I'm curious." She gave me a seductive look that had my body going crazy.

I looked her up and down, then reached for the towel, un-tucking it and revealing her nudity again. I made sure I peeped everything. She had some nice brown titties that sagged just a little bit, just like I liked. Her nipples were big and chestnut brown, and to my amazement, erect. She had a li'l stomach that was smooth and caramel. Her kitty was fully shaven with the lips thick and juicy. Her thighs were thick and her body stood on pretty pedicured toes.

I nodded my head and re-tucked her towel. "Yeah, you got a real nice body."

She shivered and shook her head before leaning in and kissing me on the cheek. "You do somethin to me,

Racine, that I don't understand. I feel like you gon' be the reason Rayjon kill the both of us."

I didn't know what the fuck she was talking about, but I wasn't afraid of Rayjon, or no nigga for that matter. In my opinion if he'd had the type of control of his woman he thought he did, she wouldn't have been hungry for my attention. I couldn't help that females found me attractive, and it wasn't my fault this nigga had a bad bitch who was feeling me. Had Kenosha been feeling him, I would have let them explore that shit. On top of that, I didn't feel like I owed Rayjon no loyalty when it came to the women aspect of things. We were strictly business partners, nothin' more. That nigga wasn't Tez, or my blood for that matter.

I grabbed Averie aggressively to me and gripped that big-ass booty, squeezing it. That muthafucka was real soft, yet firm. I cuffed it and sucked on her neck while she moaned out loudly and started to whimper like a puppy that had been left out of the house. "I ain't worried about no nigga killing me, but if I had to get buried for a reason, after seeing what you got under this towel, it'd definitely be worth it." I sucked her neck again, this time biting into it.

She dropped the towel and put her leg up on the toilet seat, exposing herself. "Please, just touch my pussy. I just want to know what it will feel like wit' you touching me down here." She grabbed my hand and placed my fingers right in between her lips. As soon as they touched her, she shrieked and started to shake uncontrollably as she fell against me.

I held her up for a second before sitting her on the toilet. I didn't know how much time we had been in there, but I knew I had to go. Getting on my knees quickly, I opened her thighs, and kissed her right on her wet pussy, opened the lips, and licked from the bottom all the way to her clit. She started to shake all over again before moaning.

I bit her thigh, grabbed the towel, and gave it to her. "You gotta get out of here, but you definitely got my attention. I don't know what type of thing you and the homie going through, but that ain't my bitness. I'm feeling you, and that's all that matters to me."

She stood up and wrapped the towel around her with a look of worry on her face. "Please don't tell him about this. He'll kill me, and then he'll kill you. Rayjon don't care about hurting nobody. I swear to God, he don't," she whimpered and stepped into the hallway. "That nigga been beating my ass ever since we left Jersey. I'm tired of it, and I just wanna be loved. Please don't tell him what we did."

I wanted to delve into what she was really going through wit' the homie, but I had already been up there for almost ten minutes, and I figured sooner or later he'd come up there trying to see what was going on. Then he'd find Averie in a towel that barely covered her private areas, and by the way she was talking, I'd probably have to body that nigga and lose out on all that paper he was lining me and Tez up wit'. I didn't like how she seemed so scared of this nigga, though. That made me feel like the homie was bullying this female, and ninety nine percent of the niggas that bullied women were low-key bitch-niggas. They were never able to stand up against real men, and I was hoping Rayjon really wasn't this type.

"Look, Averie, I ain't that type of nigga. I ain't gon' say shit. I'm feeling you, and I wanna get to know you better. I don't know what's really going on between you and him because that ain't my bitness, but you and I need to get to know each other a little better. Okay?" I said, rubbing her soft cheek.

T.J. Edwards

She nodded her head slowly, then smiled. "Racine, I swear to God, I'll put you up on some real cash, and you take time out to get to know me. I'm so trapped wit' him. I need an escape."

After saying that she jumped, and I could hear footsteps coming up the back stairs. She ran down the hallway, toward their bedroom I assumed, and I closed the door and finally got the chance to relieve my bladder. Like I said before, I didn't feel like I owed that nigga Rayjon no kind of loyalty outside of the licks we were due to hit together. That fool wasn't my blood, and he wasn't my nigga. I ain't really have no love for him or any other man, with the exception of Tez. Averie made a comment about putting me up on some real paper, and I intended on seeing what she had on her mind.

***

That same day I bought my daughter a five-foot-high Barbie Dream house that had her screaming at the top of her lungs when she saw it. "Daddy! Daddy! Oh my God, you got my house! You got my house! I love you so much!" she screamed before wrapping her arms around my legs.

I picked her up and hugged my baby girl, kissing all over her pretty cheeks. "I love you too, baby, and you deserve this, so I want you to enjoy it." I put her down and she ran and fell to her knees in front of it, opening the house up and talking to herself the whole time. I couldn't do nothing but smile.

I loved making my little girl happy. I felt like that was my job, and every single day I tried to excel at it.

Kenosha walked up and laid her head on my shoulder. "You know you be spoiling her way too much. Everything that little girl ask for, you get her. Don't you

Ski Mask Cartel

think you're creating a monster?" she asked before stepping in front of me and looking in my eyes. I moved her out of the way so I could see my li'l momma enjoying herself. I wasn't trying to hear what Kenosha was talking about. As long as I was alive, Madison was gon' get everything she asked me for. "Kenosha, stop hating on my baby before I ball yo' li'l ass up. She don't be saying shit to you when I be buying you all types of jewelry from Harry Winston's, do she?"

Madison took out the brown Barbie and hugged her to her chest. She smiled with her eyes closed, causing her dimples to display themselves on each cheek. My daughter made me feel proud to be a father. I loved Madison with all my heart. I don't think I could express that enough.

Kenosha saw the way I was peeping Madison and rolled her eyes. "Damn, I'm starting to feel like you love her more than you do me, but I know that ain't the case. Right?" She looked into my face and tilted her head to the side in question.

"I don't love nobody on this earth more than I love my daughter. You already know that." Like I said before, I had never lied to my BM before, and I refused to right then.

She bucked her eyes and gave me a look that said she was shocked before shaking her head real hard. "I know you just playing, so I ain't even finna go there wit' you right now."

Madison stood on her tippy toes and kissed the chimney of the house. "I love you so much, house!" she hollered and gave it a big hug with her eyes closed.

I smiled. "Kenosha, just because I love her first and foremost don't mean I don't love you, so let's not get into one of them arguments. That's just our child. She needs that go-hard for her ass love that I got in me, and it's my job to protect her and keep her as a child for as long as possible because that world out there is evil as a muthafucka."

Kenosha nodded her head. "Yeah, I guess. I mean, technically we are supposed to love her first, but it still hurts me when you say it like that because I never had all that you're renderin' to her, and it makes me jealous. My father was a deadbeat from day one. And I have never met a man who treats me or our child the way you do, so when I just look at the full picture of what she has, it just makes me a little jealous. It's a guarantee you will always love her the way you do right now, whereas your love for me can dwindle because I'm just your BM. That reality scared me every single day because if you chose to replace me, then what would I have in life?"

I never liked when she talked like that because, to me, that made her sound weak told me she had no self-worth, that she devalued herself. "Kenosha, that's why we signing yo' ass up for school. That way you can get you a degree and stand on yo' own two feet, because you are more than what you believe you are. I know for a fact you can do anything in this world you want to, and you don't need me. You just want me. So, we gon' find you a college and get you enrolled for the spring semester. You understand me?"

She nodded. "But just because I'm getting a degree don't mean I ain't gon' need you. Money is at the bottom of the totem pole when it comes to my reasons for needin' you." She stepped forward and wrapped her arms around my neck. "I just love you, daddy. You're everything to me."

Madison stood up and put both of her hands on her hips. "Hey, he's my daddy, not yours," she said with a frown on her face.

I couldn't do nothing but laugh.

Chapter 11

"I don't like them east coast niggas, Racine. On every-thing, cuz. You already know we ain't finna get along wit' them niggas. As soon as they get comfortable out here, they gon' think they runnin' shit, and that's when I'ma body one of them niggas, cuz. You know I already don't like no nigga, period. You the only muthafucka I jam wit', and it's because we used to take baths in the same tub, Jo. Damn," Tez said before leaning down and tooting a thick line of powder from the plate he had on his lap.

We were sitting in his living room, waiting on Rayjon to give us the call letting us know he, Vaughn, and Wood were ready to hit the Chase Bank on South Federal. It had only been a week after we'd first sat down and brought up the topic of the bank, and he felt we were ready to make shit happen. I was, too. I needed that hunnit gees just to feel somewhat secure financially. I felt like my plate was getting bigger and bigger, so I needed more chips. I still wanted to find a way to have a sit-down wit' Averie so I could see what was on her mind when it came to the large sums of money, but I hadn't figured out a way to isolate her from Rayjon.

"Cuz, you already know I don't fuck wit' out-of-town niggas, either, and I can read they faces. They ain't feeling us on that level. I don't know what Rayjon on, but I feel like when it comes down to it he gon' ride wit' them niggas over us any day because they all got his-tory. We gotta figure out a way to be smart, get our chips up, then slowly branch off from them niggas."

Tez pinched his nose and nodded. "Yeah and start our own Cartel. That shit ain't that hard once you got bread, anyway. That nigga Rayjon ain't doing shit we can't do. He just got a few plugs that we need to get, that's all."

"Dang, y'all talking about my cousin like he ain't shit," Raven said, walking into the living room holding their four-year-old son, Martez. "I thought me putting you in wit' him would be a good thing. I guessed wrong."

Tez shook his head. "That's what I'm talking about, Racine. That's why I be beating her muthafucking ass." He jumped up and snatched Martez from out of her arms as the little boy started to scream at the top of his lungs. "Huh, Racine, hold my son while I handle this bitness."

He held the little boy by one arm. I jumped up because I thought he was gon' drop him. I grabbed him from Tez and wrapped my arms around him protectively just as Tez grabbed a handful of Raven's hair and yanked her head to his chest violently.

She screamed. "Ah! Let me go, Tez. I ain't got time for this shit today. Please," she hollered and tried to free her hair from his grasp by scratching at his hand.

Tez swept his leg under her and flipped her on her back. She fell to the floor with a loud thud, her head bouncing off the carpet. I started to feel some type of way.

"Bitch, I told you about getting in my bitness, didn't I? Didn't I tell you that when I got company over you supposed to stay yo' monkey-ass out of my face?" He slapped her so hard he split her mouth immediately. Blood leaked out of the corner of her mouth and dripped down her cheek.

Martez started to cry louder, and I didn't know whether to put him in his room so he couldn't see that shit or try to pull Tez off his mother right away.

After Tez raised his hand and slapped her again, I'd witnessed all I could take. I sat Martez down and pulled Tez off Raven, whose face was covered in her own blood. "Nigga, chill. You ain't gotta be beating on shorty like that. Yo' son seeing this shit. It ain't that serious."

He frowned and pushed the shit out of me. "Racine, I done told you about trying to help this bitch when I'm getting in her ass. Now, this my ho, and if I wanna beat my bitch every single day, then that's what I'ma do because I pay all the bills in this muthafucka. You got that?" he said, walking up on me and breathing all hard in my face.

My heartbeat sped up. I didn't like nobody being in my face, especially no nigga, cousin or not. I looked to my left and saw Raven trying to get to her feet. When she stood up, she appeared dizzy and disoriented. She staggered and fell back down to one knee with blood dripping from her chin. Martez came over and tried to wrap his arms around her while he cried.

"It's okay, Racine. He right. I wasn't supposed to be in here," she said, sounding out of breath. "I was supposed to get my ass whooped."

Tez turned to his right and smacked her so hard he knocked her back to the floor. "Shut up, bitch! You still talking."

Martez screamed even louder and ran to his fallen mother.

Fuck that. That was way too much for me. I waited until Tez turned to look back at me and busted him right in his jaw super hard. *Bam!* I backhanded him, then hit his ass with a left hook that knocked him clean out, and I didn't give no fuck.

I left him there, went over to Raven, and helped her sit up before leading her to the couch and giving her a bag of ice to put on her swollen face.

"He gon' kill us when he wake up, Racine. I swear he gon' kill us when he wake up. You should have never did him like that. He gon' take that shit out on me." She slurred her words because her lips were as big as boxing gloves. Slobber mixed with blood oozed from them as she spoke. Every time I saw it, it made me want to whoop Tez's ass some more.

"Raven, just chill," I said, picking up Martez and placing him on the couch beside his mother. "I'll worry about Tez. Me and that nigga always fighting, anyway. When he wake up, we'll finish whatever he want to. This shit ain't gon' fall on you. I refuse to let that happen." I didn't give a fuck what that nigga Tez was finna be on wit' me, but I wasn't about to let him do shit to her. In my opinion, I had allowed him to do way too much already.

See, I didn't fear my cousin, or no man for that matter. I didn't give a fuck who it could have been putting they hands on a female in front of me, I would've fucked 'em over. Just because Tez was my cousin didn't mean I was gon' give his ass a pass. Never that.

Tez slowly came to his feet about ten minutes later, squinting his eyes with his hand on his head. "Fuck, what happened to me?" he asked, bucking his eyes.

I curled my lip as I stood close enough to him to bust him in his shit again if I had to. "I knocked yo' ass out because you were about to kill Raven. That powder got yo' ass doing too much. I ain't honoring that shit."

He lowered his eyes, then bucked them before pulling out his pistol so fast it caught me off guard. He pressed the barrel to my forehead and cocked the hammer. "Nigga, you knocked me out in front my bitch and my shorty. I told you about gettin' in my bitness, didn't I?" he said through clenched teeth.

I know most niggas would have been scared for their lives by having a pistol put to their forehead, but in my case it just pissed me all the way off. Not only did this nigga have a gun pulled on me, but he had that shit pressed to my head like a bitch-nigga. I didn't even

Ski Mask Cartel

think about him pulling the trigger. I don't know why. I simply smacked the gun to the side and punched him straight in the mouth, knocking him backward at the same time he pulled the trigger. *Boom!*

Raven started to scream at the top of her lungs. "Oh my God! Oh my God!"

Tez fell against the wall, leveled the gun at me, and pulled the trigger again. *Boom!* The bullet slammed into my right shoulder and knocked out a chunk of my meat. The pain was unbearable. It felt like I was being stabbed and burned with acid at the same time.

"Fuck! Dawg, I ain't mean to pop you, cuz. Fuck, that's my bad," Tez said, holding the smoking gun. He put it on his waist and walked over to me while Raven screamed in the next room.

I waited for him to get as close to me as possible before I rushed his ass, punched his ass with my left fist and tackling him into the wall as he fell backward. Then we were tussling. He head-butted me in the shoulder I'd been shot in, causing pain to shoot all over my body. Then he picked me up in the air and slammed me on my back, pulled his gun back out, and aimed it at my face.

"Nigga, calm yo' ass down. Now, I said I ain't mean to shoot you. We gotta get you some medical treatment before you bleed out."

I was angry and dizzy at the same time. The only thing that kept going through my mind was that my cousin had shot me. I wanted to get in his ass. There was no way I was gon' accept that shit lying down. Fuck that. I tried to get up again but got so dizzy I couldn't see straight. I felt my blood pourin' out of me.

I looked to my right and saw Raven holding Martez in her arms. He had a big bullet hole right in the center of his forehead with blood pouring out of it.

That was all I could take. I passed out.

When I woke up briefly, I saw Tez freaking out over his son. He had tears in his eyes, holding the boy in his arms. Then I passed back out again, and when I awoke again I saw Averie looking down on me with concern written across her face.

"Racine. Racine, are you okay? Please tell me you are okay," she said, sounding a million miles away.

I tried to sit up when a wave of nausea hit me. I leaned to the side of the couch I was sprawled out on and purged my guts all over the floor. After I was finished I lay back, dizzy as fuck and scared to open my eyes because the room kept on spinning.

I felt Averie rubbing my chest. "You gon' be okay. I already pulled that bullet out of you and stitched you up. You just lost a lot of blood. That's why you feel sick. Give your heart enough time to catch up," she said, kissing me on the cheek.

I winced in pain. "Where is Tez? Is my li'l cousin okay?" I asked, speaking in terms of Martez. I opened my eyes to see her response and understood for the first time I was in Rayjon's basement where we'd had the meeting. The room was still spinning and my head was pounding.

She shook her head. "Nall, he killed his son. The little boy is dead. They out trying to figure exactly what they should do because Raven went into shock. I feel sorry for them. What were y'all arguing about, anyway?" she asked, rubbing my chest.

I felt so sick by this time that I was finna throw up again. I dry heaved, then leaned over and threw up all over again before lying back on my back.

Averie went and got some cleaning supplies and started to clean up the mess. "Don't worry, Racine. I'll clean this shit up for you. I know you was probably protecting that girl, just judging by yo' temperament. Damn, I feel sorry for Raven, though," she said, and I started to hear her spraying the disinfectant.

I closed my eyes real tight and had a heavy heart for Martez and Raven, and even my cousin. I knew he didn't mean to shoot his only child, but now it was his reality to deal with. I wondered where he was and what was going through his mind.

After Averie cleaned up the mess, she knelt beside me and laid her head on my chest, listening to my heartbeat. "Racine, I know you out there trying to get yo' weight up, and I can put you up on some serious bread if you're willing to fuck wit' me on that level. I'm talking at least a million dollars in cash, and five hundred thousand in heroin." She looked around like she was paranoid or something.

Even though I was in a lot of pain and dizzy as hell, money was still on my mind. I tried to sit up and the pain in my shoulder started to scream bloody murder. I blinked tears. "Fuck. What you talking about, Averie?"

She stood up and ran to the stairs, looking up them and not moving, as if she were trying to see if she could hear anything. After convincing herself the coast was clear, she came back over to me and knelt down. "I got access to Rayjon's stash. I mean all of it, and I'll place it before your feet as long as you protect me and help me get away from him, because I can't take his abuse anymore. I'm tired of him putting knots on the top of my head. Feel this," she said, taking my hand and moving it around her scalp.

I could feel all kinds of lumps and knots, so much so I felt even more sick. I didn't understand what was up with them niggas and females.

"He beats me on the top of my head so other people can't see my abuse. Sometimes he does it so hard I black out, and most times I don't even deserve it. He blames me for his brother getting killed. You see, me and Rayjon's brother, Ajani, used to be together. Ajani was my son's father until both were killed. All the while me and Ajani were going through problems, Rayjon was the one who consoled me. He stepped up to the plate when his brother kicked me to the curb for my younger cousin, Stacey, and basically every other young female that would open their legs for him. Well anyway, the day Ajani was killed, me and him had got into an argument because he tried to force himself upon me, and I didn't let it happen. He stormed out of my house and was murdered that night in a sadistic fashion. Three days later we watched Rayjon's mother and father be killed by his own cousins. His family is crazy, and I had to break away from them. Ever since all their murders, he hasn't been the same. He's trying to stack up enough money so he can form an army of niggas to go at his cousins that killed his parents. They have their own cartel of killas out in Brooklyn. I know they'll be coming for our lives, and I just want to get out before they come. You gotta help me. I'll make it worth yo' while, Racine. I promise."

I tired once again to sit up. She was throwing so much at me that I could barely keep up. I tried to imagine Rayjon in my mind's eye. He didn't look as crazy to me as she was making him out to be, but then again, I was wondering why she would lie to me when she barely knew me to begin with.

"Averie, I'm wit' you one hunnit percent. I feel like we can help each other. If you really trying to get away from this nigga, and you saying you can help me get my bands up, then I say let's do this shit, because I got a daughter to feed, and ain't nobody gon' stand in the way of that. So, what are you thinking?"

Ski Mask Cartel

She bit into her bottom lip, and I noted that it quivered as she looked back over her shoulder at the stairs. That made me wonder where Rayjon really was.

She turned back to me and smiled weakly. "I'll tell you what, Racine, just let me put some things into perspective. When I get everything in motion, I'll hit you up, and that will let you know I am ready for you. I just gotta figure some shit out before I get to that place, but it won't be long. I promise you that." She rubbed my chest, then lay her head sideways on it. "What if you have to kill him for us to make this move? Would you be down for that?" she asked, rubbing my naked stomach.

I watched her fingers slide over my ab muscles. The only thing I was thinking about was the million dollars in cash and the five hunnit thousand worth of heroin. That was enough for me to get knee-deep into the game. I needed everything she was talking about to come into fruition. If I had to kill Rayjon's ass for that kind of paper, then I would just cross that bridge when I came to it. I had to make shit happen for my daughter and Kenosha. I didn't give a fuck what I had to do in order to ensure they would always be straight. I took a deep breath. "You know what, Averie? We'll cross that bridge when we come to it."

She nodded her head. "Okay, baby."

T.J. Edwards

Ski Mask Cartel
Chapter 12

Tez knelt down and lowered his son into the shallow grave with tears in his eyes. I'd never seen my cousin cry before, and it was fucking me up. After Tez accidentally shot and killed Martez, Rayjon advised against him taking the boy to the hospital because it was a guarantee he would have been arrested for first degree intentional homicide, and Rayjon felt like that would have brought down a lot of heat on our Cartel.

Raven told me Tez and Rayjon had gotten into it over that, but the result was us taking Martez's body out to the boondocks and burying him in somebody's cornfield. I personally didn't know what to feel about it. I mean, even though Martez was my li'l cousin, I really never bonded wit' him on that level, and I wished I would have. Tez seemed like he was taking the shit extremely hard, though.

It was two in the morning, two days after the accidental shooting. It was freezing outside, and it had taken us three hours just to dig a hole deep enough to put Martez's body into.

Tez lowered his son into the grave, then rocked back and forth wit' tears in his eyes. I knelt beside him and wrapped my arm around his shoulder while Rayjon, Wood, Vaughn, and Raven stood a li'l ways back from the grave. Raven had been crying ever since the tragedy had taken place. She looked worn out and exhausted. Rayjon wrapped her in his embrace and rubbed her back.

Tez shook his head. "I never meant to hurt my li'l nigga, Racine. You know I'd never hurt him like that. I feel like I can't take this shit," he said before more tears poured out of his eyes. He lowered his face to the dirt, and I could hear him sobbing.

I really didn't know how to console him because that was his child and he had killed him. I felt lost in that moment, and I did all I could to empathize with him, but the only thing on my mind was that million dollars in cash Averie had told me about. I wanted that shit. I already had plans for it.

I rubbed Tez's back. "It's gon' be okay, cuz. You know you'll bounce back from this shit. I got yo' back, nigga."

Rayjon came and knelt down beside him "Yeah, we all do. Accidents happen, li'l homie. You can't go backward. That's just a part of the game."

"I wish y'all quit talking about this situation like my whole-ass son ain't dead right now. All you niggas steady consoling him, but what about me? I'm the one that gave birth to him. I'm the one whose ass Tez was whooping when this shit happened. Fuck his feelings right now, I'm his mother," Raven said, falling to her knees beside the grave. "What am I going to do? What am I going to do without my baby?" she whimpered with smoke from the cold air coming out of her mouth every time she spoke.

I felt Tez's body go tense, then he started to shake. "I'm tired of hearing this bitch mouth, man. I said I was sorry a million times, yet she still on this punk shit." He threw me off him and hopped up so fast it caught me off guard. By the time I recovered, he had Raven on the ground with a .45 stuffed into her mouth. I could hear her gagging over the barrel.

Rayjon jumped up and pulled out a 9-millimeter, then Vaughn and Wood pulled out their guns. All of them were aimed at Tez.

"Yo, Tez. Chill, my nigga. She going through something right now, li'l homie. I can't have you killing my cousin in front of me. You pull that trigger and we gon' be forced to body you. I don't wanna do that because you my family," he said, cocking his gun.

Tez ignored him. "Bitch, you think I'm finna let you throw this shit in my face for the rest of my life? You think I'm finna go through that? Huh?" he asked her through clenched teeth.

Raven shook her head from right to left with tears pouring out of her eyes.

I didn't have no pistol on me. My shit was in the car, and I was regretting not bringing it. I was trying to figure out if I would be able to make it to the car and back without somethin' huge jumping off, but I doubted that. "Tez, come on, cuz. You just hurting right now. She ain't the enemy. You both going through something, and this ain't the way to handle it. Trust me, cuz," I said, kneeling down beside him and putting my hand on his shoulder. In all honesty, I think if I had my pistol wit' me at that time I would have popped my cousin, because to me that was bitch-shit he was on. I didn't like the fact he was trying to punish his BM for her grieving over their child and pointing out the obvious. The fact of the matter was he had killed their child, and we were consoling this nigga way too much. She was just keeping shit real.

Tez pulled the gun out of her mouth and laid it on the side of him, snatching her up and wrapping his arms around her. "I'm sorry, baby. I swear I am. I'll find some way to make this shit up to you. I promise I will."

He held her and they shed tears together for about twenty minutes straight. The whole time I was freezing my ass off, feeling the pain in my shoulder, and thinking about that million dollars.

***

T.J. Edwards

Two weeks later my shoulder wasn't feeling all that bad, and I was able to move it a lot more than I had been able to when the shit had first happened. Rayjon wanted to spend some alone time wit' Tez to get his head back right before we did the bank job, but he put a job in front of me, Wood, and Vaughn.

"Look, this move I'm gon' hit y'all wit' fifteen gees apiece to body these three li'l niggas out in Hyde Park. The reason why the payout is only at fifteen apiece is because it's a simple slaying just to make a statement to a muthafucka that's thinking about taking that stand against one of my clients. The three li'l niggas is his sons, and since he been indicted they been trying to get they weight up by using his old connects and street fame. I want y'all to hit they ass up wit' no pistols unless you absolutely have to use them. I want these li'l niggas to die by that blade or wit' they necks snapped. The more gruesome, the better. This shit gon' put our cartel on the map, take my word for it." Rayjon handed all three of us a box of army combat, nine-inch, extreme ridged blades. "These muthafuckas right here'll cut through bone if you need 'em to. The oldest boy know where his pops hid over a hunnit thousand dollars. Find out where. I don't care how you do it. Just no guns," he said as we sat in the basement of his house, looking up at him under the red light bulb.

***

The next night I found myself climbing into the living room window of their two-story, white-bricked home with Vaughn and Wood climbing in the widow after me. As I dropped to the floor, I looked around and noted it was so dark I couldn't even see in front of me. I could only hear Vaughn and Wood drop to the floor right beside me. I took my phone out of my pocket and used it as a light to guide me through the house before we agreed we would find a brother apiece and bring them into the living room.

I could hear Bryson Tiller coming out of speakers somewhere in the house, followed by what sounded like soft moans. As I got to the bottom of the staircase, the sounds got a little louder. I made my way up the stairs and was met by a narrow hallway that looked to have three doors. I sized them up quickly, then went from each one until I located the music and the now-loud moaning. It sounded like some female was on the other side getting the business.

I pulled out the army knife and, with my left gloved hand, tried the door knob, turning it until the door slowly opened. I eased it in and was met my louder moaning and the smell of sexual funk. It smelled like they had been in there fucking all day long without taking a break to wash they ass. I scrunched my nose under my ski mask and dropped to the floor, easing the door in a little more so I could slip into the room. The further I got in, the more I could hear the springs of the bed going haywire.

"Un! Un! Un! Shit! Fuck me, baby! Fuck me harder! Yes! Mm!" it sounded like a white girl said.

There was more grunting and the bed really started to go crazy, like the dude was trying to kill her ass. I looked up and saw he indeed had the white girl pushed into a ball while his black, hairy ass went back and forth into her body. The room was completely dark with the exception of a porno movie that played on the big screen.

"Ah! Oh, my fucking God! Damon, somebody is in here!" the white girl screamed and scared the shit out of me at the same time.

Damon pumped into her two more times, must've saw me, pulled out of her, and started to reach under the

T.J. Edwards

pillow she had her head on. Fuck that. I jumped up and dove across the bed, slamming the knife right into his back.

"Aw! Shit!" he groaned and fell off the side of the bed.

The white girl screamed again, this time so loud my ears started ringing. She jumped out of the bed and made her way toward the door. I turned around to chase her ass, but Damon jumped up and tackled me to the bed. I landed on my shoulder and wanted to scream louder than the white broad did. That old pain from the gunshot was back in full effect. I mean it was howling.

Damon started to grunt as he tried to gain control of the situation. "Dope-fien'-ass nigga, you gon' wish you never tried to rob my house."

He cocked back and punched me right in my jaw. I mean he rocked the shit out of me. I felt a little dizzy and everything. I took my knife and slammed it into his rib and twisted that muthafucka.

"Aw! Shit!" He fell off me and the knife came out of him.

Now I was pissed off. As soon as he fell backward, I straddled him and slammed the knife into his collar and pulled downward, ripping apart his upper left shoulder. I could feel the blade rubbing against his bone before it went back to cutting his soft muscles and tissue.

He tried to push me off him. He wiggled his waist and kicked his legs, but I wasn't going nowhere. "Aw! Fuck, man. Okay, you can have everything. Just get off me. It's two hunnit gees in the house. I'll take you to it. It's right in my closet over there."

I slammed the knife into his other shoulder and put my lips on his ear as he cried out in pain. "Bitch-ass nigga, you better take me over there, and it better be at least two hunnit gees in that safe or I'm gon' rip yo' ass to shreds wit' no mercy. Let's go!" I hollered, getting up off him.

He crawled across the floor on his knees until he got to his closet door, opening it. I had the white girl on my mind, but she was long gone. I figured we had about ten minutes to get out of that house before she went and got help, so I wanted to make the best use of my time.

Damon threw open the closet door, pushed a bunch of shoe boxes out of the way, and there, a small mini-refrigerator-sized safe appeared. It took him less than thirty seconds to pop it open. I was beside him wit' a pillowcase, snatching the bundles of cash out of the safe and throwing them into the pillowcase.

Once I cleaned the safe out, I stood up, looking down on him as he bled profusely. "What else y'all got in this house? Huh, nigga? And keep in mind I already got an idea, so don't play wit' me." Behind me, the porno movie continued to play. Two dudes were fucking a slim white girl who was moaning like she was being killed.

Damon shook his head. "That's it, bro. I swear it is. We ain't got shit else hear. That gotta be a come-up for you. Just leave, man."

I knelt down and wrapped my hand around his throat, feeling the pain in my shoulder once again. "You sure, nigga?"

He nodded his head, and I took that as my cue to handle my bitness. I took the knife and slammed it into his chest with all my might and ripped it downward. He jumped and tried to swing at me, fighting for his life, but I wasn't trying to hear that shit. I pulled it out and saw his blood drip from it before I slammed it back into his chest right where I guessed his heart would be. That nigga got to shaking as I held it there, twisting the blade before pulling it out and slamming it into the same spot again while he choked on his own blood and threw up plasma.

After I bodied him, I went into the pillowcase and stuffed as many bundles of cash into my pockets as I could. I figured when we got back into the car I could always stuff some of the money into the seats. I was trying to get at least fifty bands before I split the rest of the pot wit' Rayjon and the rest of the cartel. I was out for my daughter first. She was always at the forefront of my mind.

I ran out of the room and down the stairs. When I got into the living room I damn near had a heart attack because I got there just in time to see Vaughn holding the white girl against the wall while he stabbed her repeatedly. I literally watched the knife go in and out of her body. He must've jugged her over a hunnit times before she dropped to the carpet lifeless. I didn't know how to feel about that. I guess I was just glad I didn't have to do it to her.

Wood was carving the word 'snitch' on one of the dudes who were duct taped to chairs. Right on his forehead. I could hear him screaming under his duct tape as his skin peeled away and the bloody letters formed.

"This how we do that shit on Burleigh, kid. This a no-snitch policy. Yo' pops should have known that." He took his knife and slammed it into the man's stomach so hard it made the man blow snot out of his nose. Then the snot turned to blood. Wood cocked the knife back and slammed it into him again and again with anger. "This Burleigh Wood, muthafucka! Burleigh! The Zoo, nigga!" He stabbed him over and over again until the man's lap looked like a bloody mess.

I was ready to go. I felt like we had the money, there was no reason for us to stay there and play wit' them. I felt anxious and a little uneasy. I kept thinking about the fact there was a dead white girl on the floor. That was serious because the state of Illinois was racist as a muthafucka. If we didn't hurry up and get out of there, they were gon' fry our black asses.

Vaughn pulled the other man's neck back and held his knife in his gloved hand. "I take it that's the money right there, kid?"

I nodded my head. "Yeah, I done already emptied out they safe. We can get up outta this bitch."

"A'ight, let me slice this bitch-ass nigga up." He came around and stood in front of the other brother, pushed his head back, and started to slice him again and again across the face while he hollered into the duct tape in pain. "This that fo'-one-fo' shit, my nigga. We don't do that snitching shit!" He sliced him again and again. He stopped and carved the word snitch into his forehead, then drug the blade down the side of his face. The screaming got louder. Then he took the knife and slammed it into the man's throat, ripping it to the right, then the left, bodying him as blood spurted into the air, splashing across his black fatigues.

T.J. Edwards

Chapter 13

Rayjon counted the money again and nodded his head. "That's 225 gees right there. That's a good lick. It's five of us, so that's forty-five stacks apiece, not including that side fifteen gees for they murders. Now, in my opinion, that's good money." He counted out the appropriate amounts and set them in front of all of us while we sat at his round kitchen table.

"Yo, that nigga Tez wasn't wit' us. Why we cutting shit down the middle like that?" Wood said, mugging Rayjon as he pushed a bundle of cash over to Tez.

Tez stood up and curled his upper lip. "What's yo' deal wit' me, my nigga?" He looked like he was ready to jump across the table.

Wood pulled out his .44 and cocked it. "I got heat for crazy niggas like you, kid. Word is bond."

Tez pulled out his 9-millimeter and cocked it. "You ain't said shit, Jo. Let's shoot this muthafucka up."

I shook my head. I was over these niggas. I missed my daughter. I scooted my chair back from the table and stood up, grabbed my money, threw it in the same pillowcase, and bounced on they ass.

I didn't even make it to my car before my phone vibrated wit' Averie's number flashing across it. I picked up and got into my whip, pulling away from Rayjon's crib.

"Racine, I need to see you right now. I'm over at my aunt's house, and she 'sleep, so you can come over. Please," she whispered into the phone.

I pulled into the back alley five minutes after she texted me the address. Snow fell from the sky in big blankets of white, and the wind was blowing so hard it moved my car a little bit. When I saw her appear, I opened the passenger's door and she got in with a pink Prada scarf wrapped around her face.

"Racine, I been thinking about you like crazy. You're the only thing that's been on my mind, I swear to God," she said, taking the scarf off to reveal she had a black eye and a busted lip.

I squinted at her injuries and felt some type of way immediately. "What happened to you?" I said, assessing them. I barely touched her lip and she winced in pain.

She lowered her head. "Yesterday was my deceased son's birthday, and I was a little emotional. Rayjon don't like when I get like that, so he made me 'snap out of it,'" she said, doing air quotes with her fingers.

I rubbed the side of her face and shook my head. "I wanna help you get away from that nigga, baby. I hate niggas that beat women. I wish I could kill everyone that got down like that. You don't deserve this shit. I mean that."

And I really did. I didn't give a fuck what a female did, I never thought it was a man's right to beat them into the ground just because they could. The more I was getting to know Rayjon through the eyes of Averie, the more I was starting to lose respect for that nigga.

Averie blinked tears. "I know how I'ma get that bread up out of that nigga. I should have it for you by the end of next week, for sure. The dope, too. I had to make sure all the codes were the same today, and they are, so there's no worries. The reason I called you over here is because I needed to see you. I really missed you so bad," she said without giving me any eye contact.

I didn't know how she could miss me so bad when we were just getting to know each other, but I didn't question her about it. I felt like it was my job to make her feel better. Plus, I knew I had to do whatever it took to get that paper up out of her. I didn't know how I felt about her just yet. "I been thinking about you a lot, too,

Averie, especially when it comes to that paper. That money is life changing. It's enough to change yours and mine if I handle shit right, and you best believe I will. I need you to trust I'ma hold you down and make sure you never gotta go back through the shit you are now. I feel like you deserve so much better."

"Aww. You're always so sweet to me." She rubbed my face. "Do you think you'll be the same way even after you get all of this money?" She looked me over closely.

"Money don't make me, shorty. If it's out there, I'm gon' find a way to get it no matter if you come through or not. Like I told you before, I got a whole-ass daughter to feed, so the grind don't stop even at a million dollars. But to answer yo' question, I was feelin' you long before you brought up this lick. I like you, and I wanna support you and be there for you in every way I can be. So yes, I'll be the same way."

Averie smiled weakly. "I know you will. Something just tells me that." She lay her head on my shoulder while the heat blew out of the vents in my car. Tori Lanez sung through the speakers. "Racine, can I be honest wit' you about somethin'?" she asked, then took her head off my shoulder.

I turned to look at her pretty face as the moonlight shone through the windshield of my car. "What's that Averie?"

"The reason I called you over here is because I need you to mentally take me out of this world for a few hours. I feel like I'm emotionally losing myself, and I need to be healed." She rubbed my chest, then lay her head back onto my shoulder.

I didn't really know what she was talking about or how I was supposed to emotionally heal her, but I was down to do whatever it took. "How can I take you out

T.J. Edwards

of this world, baby?" I asked, turning my head to the side and kissing her hot forehead.

She took my hand and placed it between her legs after opening her thighs wide. I could feel the heat coming from her crotch right away. It got my motor revved up.

"My aunt in there 'sleep. I need for you to come in and conquer my body. That will help you master my mental. Please."

Ten minutes later I was sliding her panties down her thick thighs and off her ankles while Deborah Cox sang in the background, asking the question, *how did you get here?* Dropping her panties to the floor, I pulled her all the way to the edge of the bed as she leaned over and lit a big candle that illuminated the room. She opened her thighs wide. I took my nose and sniffed that pussy up before kissing the puffy lips, opening them, and licking up and down in between them.

"Mm, Racine. I want you to taste me so bad, baby. He ain't done that to me in so long. I need it, baby. I just need to be catered too," she moaned, tilting her head back and jerking when I wrapped my lips around her clit and sucked hard.

She smelled like a salty strawberry mixed with pussy. Her scent turned me on. I couldn't get enough of it. I opened her lips wider, revealing her pink and licking up and down her crease real loudly. I sucked that clit and slid two fingers into her wet hole while she humped into them, moaning with her head tilted backward. "Cum for me, Averie. Cum for me, baby. It's okay. You can cum all over my mouth. Do it, baby. I need you to do it," I said, running my two fingers in and out of her at full speed while I sucked on her clit a little harder.

She was humping into my face at full speed now. The bed rocked back and forth. She threw her right leg over my shoulder and pulled my face into her pussy. "Uhn! Eat me, Racine! Yes, baby! Eat this pussy. Eat this shit, baby. Oh, I need you so bad," she whimpered, humping her hips even faster. "Uh! Shit, I'm cumming. I'm cumming all over yo' mouth, Racine. Ooh wee!"

She started to shake so bad I got worried for a brief second, but not worried enough to stop sucking on her big clit as I wiggled out of my pants and boxers. After she came, I stood up wit' my dick rock hard. It throbbed against my belly button, the big head oozing clear gel.

She grabbed it and stroked it up and down. "I wanna taste you, baby. I wanna taste this young dick. I know you taste good." She pushed me back and fell to her knees in front of me, stroking my dick up and down, causing it to get longer and longer before she popped the head into her mouth and sucked on it hard, causing my toes to curl. I felt her tongue wrapping 'round and 'round my head, and I whimpered a li'l bit. That shit felt good.

She popped my dick out of her mouth and started to stroke it up and down again. "Tell me you love how I did that. Tell me to suck yo' dick hard, Racine. Make me do it. Please," she said, rubbing him all over her face.

I grabbed a handful of her hair and pulled it a little bit, causing her to moan loudly. "Suck this dick for me, baby. Do it now. I ain't playing wit' you. You finna be my woman, and I want my woman to suck this dick for daddy."

She looked up at me for a brief second, her eyes got bucked, and then she grabbed my dick roughly, squeezed it as tears came into her eyes. "I wanna be yo' woman so bad, Racine. Matta fact, I wanna be yo' bitch. Let me show you how I get down." She sucked my dick into her mouth, and the grip was so hot and tight I felt tingles shoot all over me. Then she got to sucking me faster and faster, taking me to the back of her throat before pulling me all the way out until my head was resting on her lips. Then she would suck me in again. It was feeling so good I knew I wasn't finna last long. I stood up on my tippy toes and got to fucking into her face at full speed, and then my balls got tight. I felt like I wanted to holler as loud as I could as my nut shot through my dick head right into her mouth.

"Mm. Mm. Mm," she moaned as she swallowed and swallowed.

My body jerked off and on. I felt like my knees were getting too weak to hold up my body. The noises she made as she slobbered all over me were driving me crazy. She stroked my dick, squeezing out all the nut into her mouth before popping it out.

"Now I want you to fuck this pussy. I want you to give me a reason to put all of that money in yo' hands. I ain't new to this shit, Racine. You gotta prove to me you're ready to be the man, and it starts wit' you conquering this pussy. So, come on," she said, sitting on the bed and opening her thighs wide. Her pussy popped out nice and chocolate. She spread her lips, and I could see how wet she was. Juices oozed out of her pink innards.

I reached down, took a condom out of my pocket, and ripped it open with my teeth, getting ready to roll him down my pipe.

"Nall, daddy. I want you in this pussy raw. I'm thirty-three years old, you in yo' early twenties. I wanna see what that fresh dick like. Beat this pussy up the right way. I wanna feel yo' heat, not no plastic."

It took me a second to say fuck that rubber because I got to thinking about Kenosha and how me and her ain't use protection. I didn't want to put her at risk by what I did in them streets, so whenever I did do somethin' I always used protection. But then I got to thinking about that million dollars, grabbed Averie's thick-ass thighs, and pushed them to her chest. Then I took my dick head and pushed him into her tight hole before long-stroking that pussy like I was pissed off. I mean I was killing that shit.

"Aw! Aw! Shit, li'l daddy. You fucking me. You fuckin' me too hard, daddy. Aw, shit!" she moaned turning her head to the side with her eyes closed tight.

My dick went in and out of that pussy at full speed. It was hot and nice and tight. Every time I went deep it felt like her pussy was sucking me in even farther. My balls slammed into her open ass hole, and the heat drove me insane. I sped up the pace even more, closing my eyes, and biting into my bottom lip.

"You my bitch, right? Tell daddy you his bitch. Tell me you belong to me now," I growled through clenched teeth. My abs were squeezed tight. The sounds of our skins smacking together was loud in the room, along with the sounds of the headboard slamming into the wall.

"Ah! Shit! I'm. I'm. I'm yo' bitch, Racine! Shit. I'm yo' bitch now. Daddy, just. Aw! Just. Keep on fuckin' me! Aw! I'm cumming!" she hollered.

I got to slamming into her as hard as I could, beating them walls loose. That shit got to feeling so good I felt myself cumming again deep within her pussy in big globs. Her walls sucked at me, milking me like crazy. I ain't gon' even lie, that shit was making me feel some type of way.

She shook under me, then opened her legs wide, pulling me down until her lips were against mine, sucking and rubbing all over my back. I pushed her away from me, flipped her onto her stomach, and bit into the back of her neck roughly, putting her right thigh onto my forearm and sliding back into that wet pussy.

"This my muthafucking pussy. You my bitch, and you gon' get daddy rich. Tell me, baby. I wanna hear that shit." I arched my back and got to beating that pussy up all over again while her big ass sat against my stomach.

"Yes, daddy. I'ma make you rich. I'ma be yo' bitch only. I submit, daddy. I submit. I swear I do. Aw shit!" she growled.

***

I got to my crib early the next morning, and I was exhausted. All I wanted to do was get into the bed and go to sleep. I had never been more tired in my life. It was six in the morning and the sun was just coming up. I crept into the crib, took my Timms off, and made my way to my daughter's bedroom, but when I got halfway there I noted the faint sound of moans. That caused me to go on high alert. I knew damn well there wasn't no nigga fuckin' Kenosha in my house. She knew way better than that, especially wit' my daughter being there.

I continued my way to my daughter's room, stopped outside of her door, and opened it a tad. There she was in her bed wit' her pink Fendi blankets pulled over her and her little night light shining in the corner of her room, right next to her doll house. I stepped into her room and walked over to her bed, leaned down, and kissed my baby girl on her cheek.

The moans got louder in the distance, which meant my daughter, if she were awake, could have probably heard the pair. Now I was pissed. I kissed Madison one more time, then slowly crept out of the room and pulled my .45 from my hip, cocking it. I had already made up my mind that whatever nigga Kenosha had in the room wit' her, I was getting ready to body his ass right in front of her. Then I was gon' take off my belt and spank her ass before I made her help me cut the nigga up and burn his body. I smiled at that. She hated when I did that type of shit. It had only happened once before, and she couldn't stomach it.

I made my way to the back of the house where my room was located. The moans got louder until I was standing outside of the door with my hand on the knob. I heard Kenosha moan out, "Yes! Yes! Yes!" before I pushed in the door and turned on the light by flipping the switch.

"Ah!" Kenosha screamed and jumped backward. Jill was between her legs with a strap-on. As Kenosha jumped backward, the fake black dick came out of her hole glistening.

Jill looked like she had been caught by her parents. "Racine, I'm sorry. I didn't mean to disrespect yo' house or nothin'. Me and her were just horny."

I was so tired and shocked at the same time that all I could do was put my pistol back on my hip. "Y'all straight, man. I ain't got no problem wit' this. Y'all just gotta keep this noise down because I could hear that shit from my daughter's room. Kenosha, you should know better," I chastised.

Her legs were still opened wide. I could see into her hole, and it was causing my shit to swell back up, but then my dick hurt a li'l bit from all of that fuckin wit' Averie.

Jill was on all fours, and I could see her naked pussy, too. That muthafucka was fat and dripping. I wanted to tap that ass, but I would have just embarrassed myself with the energy I had left. I knew I was gon' get that ass, though.

Kenosha crawled across the bed and stood in front of me. "I'm sorry, daddy. I ain't mean to. I was just missing you, and Jill just so damn lovey-dovey. She got me all riled up, and before you know it we were, well, you saw." She looked at the ground all guilty-like.

I yawned because I was becoming bored by the whole matter. I still tasted Averie's pussy on my tongue, so who was I to be mad? "Yo, like I said before, y'all good. Just hold down that noise. Kenosha, bite on a pillow or somethin'."

She nodded. "Daddy, you wanna join us now that you here?" she asked in a seductive voice then cuffed my dick through my Tom Fords.

Jill took the strap on off, lay back on the bed, and opened her legs wide, showing me her pussy and rubbing it. "Yeah, we could use the real thing. Kenosha always talking about how yo' dick game is. Well, let me see for myself." She took two fingers and opened her sex lips wide.

I looked over her entire naked body: her big titties with the brown nipples that stood erect, her thick thighs, and her fat pussy that looked like it would be lovely to park inside. I was tempted, but then Kenosha squeezed my dick so hard it was painful. He wasn't up to par. I had cum six times wit' Averie.

"I'm definitely gon' be 'bout that action later, but right now I been up for two days straight. I ain't even got the energy," I said feeling like a sucka. If I had just one ounce of energy left, I would have used it to smoke both of they pussies. That room ain't smell like nothing but pussy, and it made me mad because I wanted some of they shit.

Jill poked out her bottom lip and slid two fingers up her pussy. "You sho'? I mean, if it's like that, I'm pretty sure we'll do most of the work wit' no problem. We just need that hot dick. I mean, at least I do," she said, running her tongue over her lips.

Kenosha looked over her shoulder at her and frowned. "You know what? I don't think I'm strong enough to share my baby daddy wit' a bitch just yet,

Ski Mask Cartel

because all that stuff you saying ain't doing nothin' but making me jealous."

I laughed at that. "Yo' li'l ass silly," I said, feeling her take her hands out of my pants.

Jill took her fingers out of her pussy and looked sick. "My bad. I was just trying to get everybody in the mood. I didn't mean to overstep my bounds." She closed her legs and started to get dressed.

Kenosha softened. "Look, it ain't like that. But tonight, I think I just wanna curl up wit' him alone. I'll come holler at you once he falls asleep."

Jill grabbed her bra and brushed me as she walked past. I could tell she had an attitude, but I ain't know what to say to her, so I just didn't say nothing at all. I was too tired.

T.J. Edwards

Chapter 14

"I done kilt this bitch, Racine. I done finally kilt my baby momma. I need for you to get over here quick before I kill myself, too," Tez said before I stormed over to his pad.

He met me at the door with a bottle of Patron in his hands. He looked worn out and a little distraught. I pushed past him and into the house. "Where she at, Tez. Where the fuck she at?" I asked, already feeling sick to my stomach. I damn near had a heart attack when I entered the kitchen and saw Raven laid out on the floor with her head the size of a pumpkin and her chest cut open. There was a puddle of blood formed around her and her eyes were wide open.

I walked into the kitchen slowly and knelt down in her blood, taking her into my arms as a lone tear escaped me. "What have you done, Tez? What the fuck have you done to her?"

Tez walked into the kitchen and took a long swallow from the Patron before wiping his mouth with the back of his hand. "Every time I saw her I thought about Martez. Plus, she kept on bringing him up. I got tired of that shit, so I bodied her. I feel sick now, though." he shrugged his shoulders and took another long swallow from the bottle of Patron.

I rocked with her in my arms. "This shit is foul, my nigga. I can't condone this fuck-shit right here. On everything, I should kill yo' punk ass, because you deserve it."

He nodded his head and took another long swallow from the Patron. "That's why I called you over here. I'm finna make you kill me, nigga. I don't wanna live no mo'." He took his .44 from the small of his back and slid it across the floor. The gun landed in her blood and nearly disappeared because there was so much of it.

I grabbed the gun out of the blood, cocked it back, walked up to him, and put it to his forehead as I grabbed his neck and slammed him into the refrigerator. "Fuck is yo' last words, bitch-nigga? Make 'em good, too."

He blinked and exhaled. "Bury me a G."

I pressed the barrel of the gun harder into his forehead. "Fuck you say?" I was sure I had heard him, but I just wanted to be certain he'd said what I thought he did.

Tears ran down his cheeks. He gave me a look that said he was tired of living and wanted me to take him out of the game. "I said bury me a G, nigga. I deserve whatever you finna do to me."

He swallowed and I watched his adam's apple move up and down his throat. I put my finger on the trigger and had visions of blowing my cousin's brains all over that refrigerator. That nigga was supposed to die. I was supposed to knock his muthafuckin' head off and make him pay for the sins of Raven and Martez. And as much as I knew what I was supposed to do, I couldn't do it because I loved that nigga too much. I still saw him as a three-year-old kid in the tub wit' me.

I took the gun down and turned my back on him.

"Racine. Racine. What the fuck? Kill me, nigga. What the fuck you waiting on? I can't take this shit." He came around and stood in my face before grabbing my shoulders and shaking me. "Kill me, cuz. Come on, man. Please kill me," he said, dropping to his knees in the blood and crying tears.

I shook my head slowly and put the gun to my forehead, scratching the side of my face wit' it. I didn't know what to do. I looked down at Raven and saw the way he'd done her, and it made me wanna body his ass all over again. No female deserved what he'd done to her. As much as I wanted to avenge her death, as much as I wanted to get into my cousin's ass, I wasn't in a position to cry over spilled milk. I had to keep pressing forward. I had to maintain my focus. I needed Tez for the bank job, and I needed Tez to be around when I hit that nigga Rayjon for his stash.

"Tez, let's get rid of this body and handle this bitness wit' big homie. We'll figure everything else out later. Right now, it's all about that paper."

He crawled through the blood, picked Raven's head up, and put it on his chest. "I'm so sorry, man. I never meant to do none of this shit. I'm just fucked up in the head right now. My brain ain't right. It really, really ain't."

I couldn't even be in the bathroom when Tez sliced Raven from the top of her pubic mound all the way up to the bottom of her chest so her blood and water could run down the drain in his tub. It was the easiest way to dispose of a body. First we had to drain them and take out the internal organs, burn the organs, then chop off the limbs one-by-one, burning them, then the torso, then the neck and head. After you burned the body, you had to crush the bones to dust and pour them into the river.

Raven's disposal job only got so far as the cutting open of her midsection before Rayjon texted my phone that he was outside.

***

That next morning at eight o'clock on the dot, I ran behind Wood wit' a Tech 9mm in my hand straight into the Chase bank and watched Tez and Vaughn as they jumped over the counter and slammed their guns into the two white ladies' faces who started to scream at the same time.

"Bitch, lay the fuck down or I'ma blow yo' muthafuckin' brains out wit' no mercy!" Vaughn hollered, grabbing her by the throat and throwing her on the floor. He took his foot and kicked her in the stomach. I heard her let out a gust of air before groanin' in pain.

Tez slammed the other woman with red hair on her back, leaned down, and punched her straight in the jaw, knocking her out cold. "Fuck all that talkin', Jo. Let's get this money," he said, jumping up and moving toward the woman Vaughn had thrown to the floor. He grabbed a fistful of her hair and half-dragged her over to a four-foot-high metal cabinet. "Open this bitch," he growled at her as she cried out in pain, hands uselessly clawing at his fist tangled in her hair.

Swallowing her sobs, the woman reached with shaking fingers for a keychain on her hip. She fumbled with them for several second, making Tez growl in impatience and press the barrel of his gun tight against her temple. She let out an involuntary whimper as she finally singled out the right key and slid it into the lock. The keypad above the lock lit up, and she punched out a nine-digit code. A loud *ker-chunk* accompanied the cabinet unlocking. The door swung open so everyone could see it was filled up with stack and stacks of money.

Tez shoved her to the floor in front of an identical metal cabinet next to the one she'd just opened. "Open that bitch next, and don't take so fuckin' long!" he growled at her as he took the garbage bag out of his waistband and popped it out. "Aye, make sure I'm straight, Jo!"

I nodded. "Nigga, hurry up!" I looked to my left and saw Wood with his shotgun down the old security guard's throat. He held him by the back of the head and forced more of his weapon down his esophagus.

Vaughn whacked the first teller upside of her head with the butt of his gun as soon as she got the second cabinet open, knocking her unconscious. He popped out his black garbage bag and started throwing money inside of it. He didn't even have to ask me to cover him. I was already on point.

The bank was empty with the exception of the two tellers and the security guard. It was quiet, but it didn't stop my nerves from getting the better of me. I already knew very few niggas got away wit' robbing a bank. Them white folks didn't play about they paper. So, I was feeling like even if we got away from hitting this lick, that shit wouldn't mean we'd actually gotten away. But to me the money was too good to pass up. I had to have it.

Tez jumped over the counter with a bag full of money. "Jo, I'ma be in the car. Hurry up, nigga!" he hollered to Vaughn, who was stuffing his bag to the max.

Wood kept the shotgun down the security guard's throat. I could tell by the way his finger was wavering on the trigger that he wanted to pull it. "Yo, kid, hurry the fuck up 'fore I waste this cracker. Word is bond."

Vaughn jumped over the counter and ran with the big Hefty bag moving from side to side. "Let's go, son!" he said, running past me all the way out the door.

I slowly backed out of the door, making sure the tellers didn't get up or do nothin' out of the ordinary. As I got close to Wood, I tapped him on the back. "Let's go, bro. Fuck dude's old ass. We good." I continued to back my way out of the door, watching the whole bank.

Wood slowly pulled the shotgun out of the man's mouth and started to back away when the old guard reached for something on his waist with a lot of determination written across his face. I saw him pull out a service revolver.

"Wood! Watch out!"

Wood dropped down to his knee. *Boom!* His bullet slammed into the security guard's face and knocked half of it off and against the wall. The guard fell to the floor with his brain leaking out of the missing portion of his head.

Then the bell started to go off loud as hell.

***

"I told you niggas! I told you niggas to not kill a muthafucka unless you had to, and you fools go in there and body an old-ass white man after beating the shit out of two white bitchez! What the fuck am I gon' do now? Huh? These white folks ain't playin' about they people or they money, and we done fucked 'em over both ways," Rayjon said, pacing back and forth inside the basement of his crib.

Wood shook his head, then wiped sweat from his brow. "Yo, word is bond, you ain't see how that cracker had the ups on me. If I wouldn't have bodied his ass, he would've hit up me and Racine. Nigga, we lucky to be alive. That's what's truth." He lit a cigarette and blew the smoke to the ceiling.

"Racine, why you so quiet?" Rayjon asked me, looking down on me wit' anger in his eyes.

I shrugged my shoulders. "I get that it was a fuck-up, but it's just like he said. That old dude was finna splash us had the homie not knocked his head off. We were on our way out the door and dude thought he was finna catch us slipping, but he didn't. Life goes on." I ain't feel like going over that shit over and over again. The white man was dead. It was all over the news. We were definitely hot, and I wanted my paper. That shit Rayjon was talking about was irrelevant.

Rayjon slammed his hand down on the table so hard my apple juice fell over and spilled across the table. Everybody jumped back except for me. I let that shit run straight into my lap because I was having visions of killing that nigga right then and there. I hated loud-ass, sudden noises, and still do to this day.

"Life goes on? Life goes on? Nigga, do you know what the fuck we up against now? Huh? Do you realize every fed in the world finna be on this case until it's solved? Do you understand we hot now, nigga? That I gotta kill my connect that put me up on this move?"

He was leaning over me a li'l too close, and that shit was irritating me. I didn't like niggas invading my personal space, especially if I could smell their deodorant, or lack thereof, which was his case. I wanted to jump up and whoop that nigga, but once again I had to be smart.

"Rayjon, we had to make a move that was in the heat of the moment. I stand by that decision. Ain't no sense in sitting here crying over spilled milk. Let's move on and figure out what we gotta do next." I said that shit as calmly as I possibly could. My temper was getting hot, and I was praying it didn't start to boil. If it did, I saw myself killing every nigga in there wit' the exception of Tez and taking that money. I started to miss Madison.

Rayjon nodded his head. "Okay. Okay, li'l homie. Since this my cartel, I'll figure this shit out. But until I do, we ain't splittin' down this pot. It's too risky. These people finna be looking for some dumbass niggas to be out in these streets spending money frivolously, and I ain't finna let that shit happen. I need to make sure this money ain't marked, and I need to change this shit over. Until I do that, ain't shit moving."

Tez stood up and scrunched his face. "Nigga, you crazy as a muthafucka. You ain't finna stand on shit like that. I don't know how you niggas get down in Jersey, but this Chicago, nigga. And after we hit licks, that shit get busted down. I put the work in, now I'm finna get paid, or we about to have a big-ass problem in this muthafucka."

Vaughn adjusted his glasses on his face and stood up. "Yo, this nigga always got somethin' to say. Nigga, don't you know how to follow rules, muthafucka? Chief said ain't shit happening until he turn that money over. That's how it's finna be. Word is bond. Back in Jersey we honor the nigga that's feeding the cartel, so fuck Chicago, nigga!"

He said that shit wit' so much venom that he spit on my arm. I already had apple juice in my lap. That shit pissed me off. I jumped up. "Nigga, fuck you! Fuck you talking about then, nigga? I'm tired of you acting like you hard, anyway. Like we don't get down in the CHI. My word is bond, we ain't honoring shit you niggas talking about."

Wood upped two .44s out of the small of his back just as me and Tez upped our 9mms and Vaughn upped a .45. "Y'all ain't finna be coming at my zoo-nigga like that. We can turn this bitch into a blood bath, word is bond."

Rayjon waved his hand through the air while we all looked at each other wit' pure hatred. "Y'all chill the fuck out. Regardless of how you feeling, we still all family. Nigga's just frustrated right now because I said what I said. It is what it is. Put them guns away or pull the triggers." He upped two .40 glocks out of the small of his back and aimed them from Wood and Vaughn to me and Tez. "Now, we gon' all kill each other. But it's blood in, blood out my nigga. We live for each other's blood in this cartel. "

I lowered my gun after sucking my teeth loudly. Them niggas ain't want no smoke like that, and in my mind it was an easier way to make shit happen. There was no way I was gon' allow this nigga to hold all of that money like that. He definitely wasn't my pimp that he could be holding my cash for me. Fuck that. I was a man, and a man didn't allow no nigga to hold his paper for him. I was finna hit this nigga real hard now, and I was gon' use his bitch to do it.

Tez cocked his pistol and lowered his eyes. "You got me fucked up, Rayjon. You not finna keep all that money like that and think it's sweet. I came to get paid, and I can't get paid if all the money is in yo' pocket."

Rayjon smiled weakly. "Tez, this money ain't going nowhere, li'l homie. I'm just gon' sit on it for a minute until I can make sure them serial numbers on them ain't being tracked. Once I confirm that, your share is yo' share. Until then, I'm gon' give you niggas thirty thousand apiece out of my own pocket.

Tez lowered his gun. "A'ight, now that's more like it. I thought you was finna leave us assed out wit' nothin'. I'll settle for thirty right now, but I'm sweating you every day until I get my cut."

After we left out of Rayjon's basement, that nigga Tez snapped out as we rolled away in his truck. "I hate them east coast niggas, Racine. On my momma, Jo, I wanna fuck them niggas over in a major way. How the fuck this nigga gon' give us some crumbs when we got a whole-ass bag of money? I ain't wit' this shit, my nigga. On my momma, I say we kill them niggas and say fuck that cartel. Let's start our own shit. You know that's how we get down in the CHI, anyway. We invented gangs and mobs."

I was feeling everything Tez was saying. I was just trying to put shit into perspective in my head. "We gon' start our own shit, and that nigga ain't finna keep that money. He just think he is. I wanna body them Jersey niggas just as bad as you do, but we have to use our smarts that this land we grew up on taught us. I got this shit, though." I was sure of that.

Tez kept on sniffing his snot back into his nose. I could tell he was getting sick, and I ain't want him to spread that shit to me. I didn't like getting sick, especially when I was trying to handle bitness.

"I hope you do, Racine, because I'm giving that nigga three days. Three days before I run up in his shit wit' guns busting and take what's mine and yours. That's on my momma, nigga."

***

Later that day, I snatched my daughter up as she was coming down the hallway and wrapped her into my arms while she screamed all loud and playful.

"Daddy! Daddy! Let me down, you big doodie head," she said, laughin' so hard her dimples popped up on her cheeks.

I carried her to my bedroom and lay back on the bed with her in my arms. "Baby girl, I love you so much, and you are the most special little girl in all of the world to me. Everything I do in this life is for you, and you first. Do you understand me?"

She squeezed my nose and made a honking sound, then started laughing. I ain't even gon' lie, that irritated me a little bit because my next move was going to be serious. I jerked her a little bit to get her attention and let her know I was serious. "Baby, listen to me, because I need you to remember these words just in case daddy don't come back home for a while."

She turned her head to the side and looked sad. "But why wouldn't you come back? Are you mad at me?" She looked like she was ready to cry.

I sat up and made her stand in front of me, holding her by the arms. "Baby, I will always come back if I can, and Daddy can never be mad at you. You're my little angel and the most special girl in the whole wide world. I just want to make sure you are always happy and have everything you need for as long as I am alive, because you are my little girl. Daddy just has a dangerous job, and he always wants to let you know he loves you before he goes to it. I love you, Ms. Dimples."

She batted her eyelashes at me and smiled shyly. She did that every time I called her that. "But Daddy, I don't want you to go. Can't you just stay wit' me, and play wit' me today?"

I smiled. "Sure, baby. Daddy'll stay wit' you all day long. I promise."

And that's just what I did. I spent the day spending quality time wit' my daughter. Whatever she wanted to do, we did it until she wore herself out and fell asleep on my chest.

T.J. Edwards

Chapter 15

I took Jill to the Chicago Bulls versus Cleveland Cavaliers game the next night, just as I promised her I would. We got there just as the game was kicking off because, when it came down to the United Center, I had learned from past experience it was better to get there right around the time the game was going to start, or even a little later because if you didn't, you'd find yourself stuck in big-ass crowds. I didn't like people rubbing all up against me, plus Chicago was well known for many pickpockets. So, we got there just as the game was starting and took our seats about thirteen rows back. The place was packed, and I was looking forward to having a good time.

Jill sat down with her nachos and hot dog. "Oh my God, I see him. I see him. I can't believe I'm actually seeing LeBron. This is the best day of my life." She rubber-necked so she could get a better look at the floor.

I smiled and took a sip of my Pepsi through the straw. Even though I fucked wit' LeBron, I never was the type to get all excited by seeing another human being, though it was cool to see him doing his thing. I was silently hoping he was about to put in work on our city's Bulls. "I just want you to enjoy yo' self, li'l momma, because you deserve that."

She took her eyes off the court and turned to look at me. "Racine, I swear I love yo' ass already. You really are a good man. I hope I didn't lose your respect by what took place between me and Kenosha. We were just on some horny shit, missing you. You know how that go."

I watched LeBron throw the ball to Dwyane Wade just to get it back and dunk on the Bulls' center. He beat on his chest and started to run back on defense. I smiled at that. To me, that nigga was a beast.

T.J. Edwards

I shook my head. "Look, Jill, I ain't sweating that stuff. Y'all are grown. If I felt like you disrespected me in any fashion, I would have let the both of y'all know that right away. But you didn't, so you good." I put my arm around her. "Just enjoy yourself. Don't you like the Prada dress and heels I bought you? Ain't you feeling these pink diamond earrings in yo' ear?" I asked, touching her earlobe.

She smiled and touched the earring in her left ear before nodding. "Yeah, you do got me looking all good and shit."

"That's what I'm saying, baby. If I felt some type of way about what y'all did, I wouldn't have never dropped these chips on you. I'ma take Remy shopping, too, this Friday when I take Madison. I think it's time I get her right. That way you ain't gotta be so worried about how you gon' figure things out for her. I got that."

LeBron was fouled so hard he fell to the floor and needed Love to come over and help him up. Then he went to the line and adjusted the rubber bands on his wrists, before getting the basketball to shoot his free-throws.

Jill looked at me for a long time without saying a word, then she leaned over and kissed me on the cheek before putting lips to my ear. "Racine, it's hard out here for a woman in my position, but because of you things have been okay. I appreciate all that you do for me and my daughter. I appreciate you, and I'm going to pay you back one of these days. I love you." She kissed me again on the cheek.

I smiled. "You good, li'l momma. Now, once again, sit back and enjoy yourself. I got you, and as long I'm here, you gon' be straight. And so will Remy."

She bit into her bottom lip, looking all sexy and shit, nodded, then turned to watch the game while I scanned the crowd for enemies. It was a sold-out event, so there

Ski Mask Cartel

were all types of people there from celebrities to the average Joe. I wished I had brought some binoculars because I liked to know who all was around me. I figured that wit' all of them people in that place, I'd have to have robbed or shot at least one of them at some point in my life. And if I hadn't, I was sure Tez had because that nigga was worse than me when it came to that jacking shit. That day I couldn't locate any enemies, so I just lay back and enjoyed the game wit' Jill, hugged up wit' her like she was my woman or somethin'. I was trying to make her feel good and appreciated after all she had been through. I felt like she deserved at least that.

After the game was over, I paid the event staff $200 apiece to let us stand in the tunnel where the players came out, and Jill was able to get Lebron's autograph on a jersey we'd bought and a Cavaliers cap. She was so excited she couldn't stop smiling and hugging me over and over again.

After we got back home, we sat in my whip for a full hour before getting out of it. In that time Jill let me know what was on her heart.

"Look, Racine, I know I don't have shit to offer you, and I know you'll probably never look at me as being up to par to be a part of your inner circle, but I just want to let you know I really do love you. And if you gave me the chance, I would really ride for you and do whatever you told me to do, even if it put my life on the line, because I know you would always lead me in the way that's in me and my daughter's best interest. Kenosha told me she ain't never had to worry about nothing ever since she was in the ninth grade, that you been making it happen ever since then, and I'm jealous because no man has ever thought to try wit' me. If you just give me a chance, Racine, I'll give you my all. I don't want to be yo' main woman. I just want to be owned by you in some sort of way. Is that possible?" She put her hand on my thigh and squeezed it.

I grabbed her head and placed it on my shoulder as I watched the snow fall against my windshield. I felt some type of way about Jill because she seemed so vulnerable, so in need of that manly love. I felt like she'd been hurt so much she really didn't know what real love felt like coming from a real man. I didn't know where I wanted her to fit in my life, but I knew I wanted her there because I wanted to make sure she and her daughter was well taken care of.

I kissed her on the forehead. "You can be my li'l boo thang. Just always keep shit one hunnit wit' me and play yo' role, and we'll figure this shit out. I care about you, ma, and I only wanna see the best happen for you and Remy. Okay?" I lifted her head off my shoulder so I could look into her eyes.

She blinked and a tear fell down each cheek. "That's all I ask for, baby. That is enough for me."

I didn't even get a chance to walk inside my crib before my phone vibrated wit' a text from Averie telling me to get to her aunt's crib right away because she needed me. My brain got to going all over the place. I didn't know what to think, but of course I started to think that somethin' was wrong, so I texted and asked her if there was a problem. Her reply was for me to get there as soon as possible.

I pulled up thirty minutes later even though her aunt's house was only regularly ten minutes away from mine, but the roads were so bad my whip kept slipping and fishtailing at every turn, so I got there as fast as I could without running into something. I jumped out of the car, ran through the backyard, and thought about beating on the door but decided against it for fear of waking up her aunt or anybody else who could have

Ski Mask Cartel

been in the house. So, instead of doing all of that, I texted her.

A minute later she opened the back door, ran out to me, and wrapped her arms around my neck. "I missed you so much, baby. I can't believe how much I need you already." She hugged me tight, then took a step back. "Come in. I wanna show you somethin' that's gon' make you real happy."

Once again, my mind was getting the better of me. For some reason I felt like I was walking into a trap. I don't know why I had that feeling, but I just did. I allowed her to walk ahead of me, and I sent Tez a quick text letting him know where I was and that somethin' didn't feel right to me. I don't know why I didn't opt to turn around and just holler at her in the car or somethin' until my brain stopped getting the better of me, but I didn't. I followed her into the house to see what was good.

It was about midnight around this time. The house was almost completely dark with the exception of a few lamps we walked past on our way through the living room and up the stairs. When we got to the second floor, Averie took my hand and led me through the first bedroom door after putting her finger to her lips. "Shh. You gotta be quiet because my aunt is down there sleeping. We don't wanna wake her ass up because she's so nosey." She turned the knob on the bedroom door and started to push it in.

I didn't know what the fuck she was talking about. My paranoia senses were tingling like crazy. I wanted to ask her why she was being all secretive, but when the door opened and I was able to look onto the bedroom, my eyes got so big they hurt. Right there before me was stacks and stacks of money. I mean, the whole bed was filled up, with the pillows on the floor to make room.

I looked down at her and she was looking up at me, smiling. I walked over to the bed and grabbed a bundle of cash, flipping through it. It was all hunnits and fifties. Now I was smiling.

"I told you I would make shit happen for you, daddy. I told you I would get you right. Now, don't I deserve at least a kiss?" she asked, coming to me and wrapping her arms around my neck.

I grabbed her and tongued her ass down with my eyes open, the whole time looking at all that money. I ain't have time to be on that lovey-dovey shit, although I would definitely give her what she had coming. After the kiss, I stepped out of her embrace and looked around. "Where the bags at? We gotta get this shit out of here. And where is Rayjon?"

She knelt down and pulled two empty duffel bags from under the bed, tossed me one, then started to load up the other one. "He had to make a run to Indiana. He gon' be back in the morning, and we need to be long gone from here because that nigga gon' lose his mind when he checks these safes."

She was breathing hard and moving around super fast. She almost tripped, and that made me look down at her feet. For the first time I noted there were about ten kilos on the floor. "What's that?" I asked, pointing and stuffing the last bit of money into the duffel bag that would fit. There was still a whole half of the bed full of cash.

She looked down. "That's the heroin. You should be able to get a hunnit a pop off them. You told me to take everything, so I literally hit his ass for everything. Most of this is from the bank you guys hit, too."

She continued to stuff her bag. When it wouldn't take any more money, I said fuck it and wrapped the rest of it in a sheet before tying it into a knot. "Come on, let's get the fuck up outta here," I said, walking toward the door and pulling it open with a duffel bag on one shoulder and the sheet full of money on the other.

"Baby, just go take that to the car, then when you get back grab that dope and I'll bring this money. You sure we're doing this though, right?" she asked, looking up to me from her one knee as she wrapped the kilos up in a sheet like she'd seen me do wit' the money.

I don't know why she asked me that dumbass question. It seemed a little odd to me, but my mind was racing so fast I could barely think straight. "Hell yeah, so hurry up."

I opened the door all the way and stepped out into the hallway, creeping down the dark stairs as slow as possible so I wouldn't make enough noise to wake up her aunt. When I hit the bottom landing, I sighed wit' relief and made my way through the living room to the back door. As soon as I opened it, the frigid air hit my face with a vengeance. It made my eyes water.

I ran through the snow in the backyard until I got to the alley where my car was parked, popped the locks, opened the door, and sat all that shit on the backseat before jumping back out, getting ready to make my way back into the house.

As I was getting out of the car, I could see Averie coming through the backyard with the rest of the money and dope. She looked like she was carrying way more than she could handle.

I got ready to run to her so I could help when I saw headlights turn into the alley, then a car came speeding down it before slamming on its brakes, causing the car the slide before it came to a halt. And that's when Wood jumped out of the passenger's seat with a MAC-11 in his hand, followed by Vaughn who had a MAC-10 in his. They slammed the doors of their car so hard it shook the vehicle.

T.J. Edwards

Wood frowned and aimed his MAC right at me while Vaughn aimed his at Averie. "I knew we couldn't trust this bitch-ass nigga or that ho right there. Ain't no loyalty in you Chicago niggaz."

Before I could even reach for my gun-,

BOOM! The fire spit from his toolie, catching me completely off guard.

To Be Continued...
Ski Mask Cartel 2
Coming Soon

Check out a preview of Bloody Commas by T.J. Edwards

Chapter 1

"*Aarrrggghhhh! Aarrrggghhhh*! Please no! Please don't kill him!" Tammy screamed, as Ajani picked Black up into the air, slamming him down on his neck. He crouched down, picking him up again, this time punching him straight in the nose, causing blood to spurt across his face.

"Bitch nigga, this shit ain't a game. Now you gon' tell me where dem birds at or I'm finna kill you, your baby and that punk ass bitch over there," he pointed at Tammy, who held their three-year-old son.

"Ajani, that's your uncle! What the fuck are you doing?" she cried.

Wham!

Rayjon took his pistol and smacked her across the face so hard with it, she flew outta the chair, dropping the little boy.

She was laid flat on her stomach, knocked out cold. A pool of blood formed around her mouth. Their little son looked up from his knees, with his hands over his ears screaming at the top of his lungs.

"Punk ass bitch!" Rayjon hollered. He got tired of her whiny ass voice. It got to irritating him, so in his mind, the only solution was to knock her the fuck out. Next, would be the little kid. Cousin or not, he didn't give a fuck. He felt no love toward him, Black nor Tammy.

"Rayjon, shut his bitch ass up, too. All that muhfuckin' noise givin' me a headache," Ajani said to his older brother, as he flung Black down into the metal chair and began taping his wrist behind his back.

"Mommy! Mommy! Peez wake up, mommy!" Lil' Black whined. He had already pissed himself. He knelt down beside his mother and ran his hand over her back. He wondered why she went to sleep after his cousin had hit her and she had an owie on her lip now. He started to cry again. This time louder than before. His wails echoed off of the walls of the sticky basement.

Rayjon scooped him up from behind, and put him into the sleeper hold. Tightening his grip every second while the boy wiggled his legs, and struggled to breathe. The more he gagged, the harder Rayjon squeezed until the little boy stopped moving all together. Then he dropped him on top of his mother. They both laid in a pile knocked out. Rayjon smile looking down on them, as Ajani tossed him the duct tape.

"This fucked up, man. Y'all ain't gotta do this shit," Black spat, as a thick rope of blood dripped of his chin. He was extremely dizzy and the room felt like it was spinning in circle. He also couldn't feel any feeling in his toes ever since Ajani dropped him on his neck. "Y'all my nephews. Cuz, we s'pose to be family."

Wham!

Ajani backed handed him with the .40 Glock. "Where dem birds at?" He wrapped his fist into Black's wife beater, and swung the toolie again.

Wham!

Splitting open his forehead, blood ran down his cheek almost immediately, and this only excited Ajani.

"*Arrrggghhh!* Nephew, awright! Awright! Nigga, you ain't gotta keep fuckin' me up." He spat out three teeth that bounced off of the ground. "Go in my son's room and move his dresser. As soon as you do that, look down and it's gon' be a hole in the bottom of the wall. Stick your finger in there and pull outward. When you do that, the whole wall will fall inward. Just look inside and them bricks gon' be right in there, cuz. Y'all can have dat shit, just leave me and my family alone," he whimpered.

"Rayjon, you heard that shit, big bro?" Ajani asked, not even taking the time to look over his shoulder at his brother. He was disgusted by how bitch-made Black really was acting.

He'd been on more than a few robberies with him where Black was the predator. During those times, he acted all hardcore and shit. Like he was really about dat life, period. Now that he was on the receiving end, he was acting like a whiny bitch, and it was pissing Ajani off.

He'd already made up his mind that he was going to kill his father's brother because, to him, that soft shit was a disgrace to the family's blood line.

"Yeah, I'll be back." Rayjon looked over at Tammy and his younger cousin once more before disappearing up the stairs that led to the main portion of the house, in search of more merchandise.

"Why y'all doin' this shit, Ajani? The fuck I do to y'all to make y'all niggaz turn on me?" Black questioned faintly, barely able to breathe, as blood continued to ooze from the slit in his forehead and spill from the place in his gums that once secured his two front teeth.

Frowning, Ajani crouched down in front of him. "You a rat, bitch nigga. My ol' man told me about the wire yo snitch ass wore while y'all conducted bidness in 'nem streets. In my eyes, you ain't nothin' but a rodent. It's time for extermination."

Black coughed up a blood loogey and attempted to spit it out, but it was so thick that it got caught on his lip and slowly crept down his chin.

"I ain't snitch on yo pops, lil' nigga. And I ain't never wear no wire," he lied.

Quiet as it was kept, he'd been working with the Feds for three months before his brother had got indicted. He was warned that had he chosen not to cooperate, he would have been indicted directly after his brother was snatched up.

Caught between a rock and a hard place, he decided to take the deal. Along the way, the Feds agreed to let him keep all of the dope they'd come up with on their licks, as well as half the cash.

"Yo, Black, on some real shit, yo best bet is to take this shit like a man, 'cause you acting like a real bitch right now. We got a whole list of niggaz that need to be brought to justice. I'm hoping they all don't bitch up like you." He shook his head in disgust.

"So, you sayin' you gon' kill me anyway?" He whimpered, smelling like he was damn near ready to shit his pants. "But I just told your brother where the dope and everything at. What more do you want from me, cuz?" Tears of panic burned his cheeks.

An infuriated Ajani lunged his leg forward, *doom* kicking Black dead in his chest, causing him to flip backwards out of the chair and Ajani to land on his ass. Jumping onto his feet, Ajani walked over to Black, looking down at him with a devilish smirk, cocking his banger back. "Nigga, on my blood, if you don't quit crying like a pregnant broad, I'ma knock yo shit off yo shoulders."

Black twisted on the ground, struggling to breathe. Ajani had managed to kick the wind out of him, making him feel as if he was slowly dying. He knew that one of his ribs had to be broken.

"Uhhhh shit! Help me! Somebody, please help me," Tammy moaned, trying to get up from the ground, as nausea consumed her body. Her jaw felt like it'd been hit by a school bus.

Ajani ran over to her, yanked her up by her hair and, with all his might, slammed the barrel of his gun into her cheek ripping her skin and breaking her jaw. "You got on the stand and testified against my Pops, bitch, and shit ain't have nothing to do with you."

"Ajani, I was just doing what my husb…"

Boom!

The bullet entered her cheek, punching a chunk of her brain out of the back of her head, with Ajani still holding her by her hair. Aiming the gun at the hole that was created, he fired off another round.

Boom!

Knocking out more of her noodles. Her body jerked violently, then he let her fall to the ground.

"Punk bitch!"

Black struggled to break free. He tried his best to get his hands loose, but the duct tape was too strong. All he'd managed to do was rock his chair from side to side. "You ain't have to do that shit, nephew. What the fuck done got into you?"

Boom!

Ajani felt the jerk of his gun as it popped a bullet through the head of his little cousin. Lil' Black's brains splattered onto the concrete floor.

He then knelt down, searching for a pulse, that was faint. He was preparing to pull the trigger once more, but the pulse flat lined.

He had no remorse. The way he saw it, Black and Tammy were both snitches, which meant their son had it in his DNA to turn out just like them.

Ajani felt like he was doing the world a favor by wiping him out before he could take after his snake ass parents.

Witnessing Ajani brutally blow his son's head off, Black's worse nightmares were confirmed. It was only a matter of time before he was next on the hit list. Had he turned the Feds down, he would have only had to serve 60 months, like his brother. But his unwise decisions had cost his family their life. He felt like a straight bitch, welcoming the thought of death.

Rayjon ran down the stairs with a .45 in his right hand and a black garbage bag in his left. When he got to the bottom landing, he looked around the basement smelling the heavy aroma of gunpowder. He saw that Tammy and Black Jr. had been murdered by his brother. He wondered what they had done to set him off, but he remembered that it never took much to set Ajani off. His temper was horrible and murder was second nature to him ever since he'd witnessed their father body a nigga in front of him at the age of eight.

"Bro, did you find that shit?" Ajani asked, grabbing Black by the back of the neck.

Rayjon picked up the bag and swiftly walked over to Ajani, kneeling down and opening it. "Yeah, it's ten keys in this mafucka, pure Cola. I ain't find no money, though. And I know if this nigga got kilos in the wall, that it's money somewhere in this fuckin' house."

Ajani put the gun to his eyes and forced it harshly into the socket. "Yeah, nigga, he got a point. Where the fuck the money at?"

Black swallowed. "Any way it goes, you lil' niggaz gon' kill me, so what's the point?" He passed gas and tried to imagine what it was going to feel like dying.

He prayed it wasn't painful and that there was an actual afterlife.

In that moment, he wanted to pray, but was afraid of which God to actually pray to because he didn't want to get it wrong. He started to panic all over again.

Rayjon scrunched his face and walked over to him after pulling his lighter out of his pocket. "Oh! You *want* us to torture yo ass, huh? You wanna go out like a G?" He shook the latter up and down. "Aye, bro, grab me some lighter fluid. I saw some in the hallway right next to their barbecue grill."

Ajani nodded his head hard. "Hell yeah! That's what I'm talkin' about. Let's burn his bitch ass into dust!" He disappeared up the stairs.

Screams of terror threatened to escape Black's mouth. The last fate he wanted to experience was death by fire. He knew that would be complete torture, pain that he could not withstand.

"You know what, Black, I never liked yo bitch ass anyway. I used to peep how you looked at my mother every time my father turned his back. You a straight snake nigga and I'm gon' enjoy bodyin' yo ass."

Ajani came down the stairs and tossed the lighter fluid to Rayjon. "Drench that bitch ass nigga and let's get the fuck outta here. That nigga can either come off them chips and take two to the head or we can burn him to death and right before he dies, give him two to the head, that's up to him."

Shrugging his shoulders, Rayjon began to pour the fluid all over him until the entire bottle was emptied of its contents, then he handed it to Ajani. "Throw that in the bag and we'll get rid of it later. Even though we got gloves on, we can't be too careful." He took a step back from Black. "So, what's it gon' be, nigga?"

Black couldn't believe his fate. He had been one of the killers that trained and introduced both Rayjon and Ajani into the game alongside their father, Greed. Now, here he was on the receiving end. *Life truly was a bitch,* he thought.

He had visions on taking the easy way out with the two bullets straight to the head, but then there was the stubborn part of him that refused to bow down to lil' niggaz and give up his money. There was an intense battle going on in his mind.

"Oh, really?" Rayjon smiled with a devious grin plastered on his face. "This nigga think it's a game."

Ajani stepped forward and taped his mouth. "We finna smoke yo ass, nigga." He stood back in amazement, barely able to contain himself. Adrenaline had kicked in. He had a deep hatred for his uncle that brewed inside of him. "Kill that nigga, bro!"

Rayjon sparked his lighter, setting his uncle on fire and returned the lighter to his pocket. He could smell the cooked skin almost immediately.

"Ahhhhhhh!"

Ajani took his blunt and lit it off of the flames coming from his uncle. He heard him hollering through the tape. Then he fell on his side while the fire ate away at him.

T.J. Edwards

Chapter 2

"Father in the name of Jesus, we pray that you bless this food, and that you protect us from any impurities. Thank you for blessing us with the provisions to do right for our family. Amen," Jersey said, praying over the food, as she held her sons' hands.

"Damn, Momma. You threw down, didn't you?" Ajani said, eyeing the food, placing two chicken breasts on his plate.

Rayjon elbowed him in the ribs. "Bro, watch yo mouth in front of Momma. You keep slippin' with that."

"Don't tell his ass nothing. He gon' understand when I crack him in the head with one of my skillets." She scooped some baked macaroni and cheese onto her plate, as she mugged her youngest son, who sat across the table looking like his fuckin' father.

They had the same build and everything. Ajani was just shorter than him. He was only about 5'10", whereas his father was 6'2". They were both 190 pounds, with the same dark brown eyes and dimples on each cheek that fooled most because their tempers were lethal.

"Dang, my bad, Momma. You know sometimes I be forgettin' to leave that kinda talk in them streets," he said, taking the bowl of baked macaroni and cheese from her.

It was Sunday and since the day they were born, it had been law for them to sit down at the dinner table as a family. Regardless of what was going on in their lives, they always found a way to make it home to enjoy their mother's dinners.

"Yeah well, you better get it together. Your brother shouldn't have to keep remindin' you how to behave in front of me." She put two drumsticks onto her plate, drenching them in hot sauce.

Rayjon spooned macaroni into his mouth. "If I gotta remind him every time, it don't bother me. We suppose to respect you more than anybody walking the face of this earth. That's what Pops always say."

Jersey smiled, gazing at her oldest. He was about 6'3" and couldn't have weighed more than 175 pounds, slim. While Ajani looked just like their father, Greed, Rayjon was damn near her facial twin. But as handsome as he was, she knew that her oldest was a no-nonsense killer.

"Yeah, you right, Rayjon. That's my bad, Momma. You know I respect you more than that." He felt horrible and prayed that his mother forgave him. She was his heart and there wasn't anything in the world that he wouldn't do for her.

"Do I gotta show y'all how to cook up one of them kilos or do y'all got it?" she asked, pouring red wine into her glass. "Since y'all ain't take time out to get no money, your father said y'all gotta hit the ground running right away. It's all kinds of bills coming up shortly that gotta be paid."

Rayjon shook his head. "Nall, we gon' go over to my crib as soon as we leave here and get right to business. You know we was raised better than that."

Jersey nodded her head. "That's what I thought."

Four hours later, they were sitting in front of a half brick of rock cocaine. Ajani took a Philip's screwdriver and slammed it in the middle of the brick, pulling it toward him. The cocaine cracked and slowly broke into big pieces. Ajani grabbed about 4 ounces, took his razor blade and started chopping up 20 pieces.

Rayjon leaned his head down and tooted up a thick line of cocaine that was still in its powder form. He hit both nostrils before joining Ajani at the table with his own razor blade.

He felt the high take over him immediately. His heart began to pound in his chest, and a strong sense of euphoria came over him. He started bagging up fat ass 20's, while Yo Gotti blared out of the radio's speakers.

"I'm about to snatch up August and Aiden and put them lil' niggaz down wit us. Them Blood niggaz tryna snatch up

Ski Mask Cartel

every young nigga from the hood and make 'em pledge their loyalties to 'em, but the way I see it, if we can grab a couple grimey lil' niggaz out da hood to fuck wit us, then we can lay this whole mafuckin' city down." Rayjon curled his lip. "That dope boy shit ain't never been my thing. I rather make a mafucka suck on this hammer and take about thirty G's in less than thirty minutes than to hustle for a whole month and make halfa dat. Shit just seem ass backwards to me." He dropped another rock into a baggie, tying the end into a knot.

"I love fast money and I love slaying niggaz. I ain't got no muthafuckin' patience. And I gotta have everything toppa the line. For me, jacking niggaz is the only way." Ajani stated, bagging dubs so fast that it left his brother in awe.

Rayjon sped up his pace. Quiet as kept, the two competed with everything they did. It was something that had taken place between them ever since Ajani was two years old and Rayjon was five years old. They were exactly three years apart, sharing a birthday.

They heard keys jiggling into the lock of the front door. Both brothers scooted away from the table and upped their heat.

Ajani cocked his back after flipping it off safety. He put his back against the wall, curling his upper lip, prepared to pop a nigga dome.

Rayjon crouched down and cocked back his .44 Desert Eagle. He lightly touched the trigger, activating the red beam on top of the gun. They ran into the front room and ducked down on the side of the door, ready to body any mafucka that came through it.

Camryn turned the lock and pushed the door open, while trying to juggle the big bag of groceries that she had stupidly got placed into a brown paper bag. It felt like it was ready to bust open, plus her arms were killing her. As soon as she pushed the door all the way in, she felt an arm wrap around her neck, then she was forced into the house after dropping the bag in the doorway.

Ajani picked her up and threw her inside. Stepping through the groceries and slamming the door behind himself, he pointed the gun at her, prepared to pull the trigger. "Bitch, who the fuck is you?" he questioned.

Rayjon jumped up and ran in front of the gun. "Yo, chill, lil' bro. Dis my woman right here."

Camryn was about ready to have a heart attack. Her high yellow face had turned beet red. She was scared out of her mind. She had never had a gun pointed at her before and the snarl on the man's face that brandished it looked cold hearted. He looked like he wanted to kill her just because he could.

"Please don't kill me. I'm beggin' you," she whimpered.

"Yo, you good, Camryn. I got dis." Rayjon said, helping her get to her feet.

Ajani put his steel back at his side. "Bro, you shoulda told me that hoez got keys to yo crib and shit. I was finna blow this bitch head right off on the porch." He shook his head and pointed at the high yellow beauty. "Bitch, you lucky."

After cleaning up the groceries, Ajani grabbed the remainder of the unbagged kilo and bounced. Rayjon stepped into his bedroom and slid his pistol under the pillow, as Camryn took her place on the edge of the bed with her head down, holding the back of her neck.

Rayjon sat down beside her and moved her long curly hair out of the way, kissing her on the neck. "What's the matter, baby?"

She felt his thick lips suck her neck and immediately tingles shot down to her nipples, causing them to spike up. He licked her ear lobe before darting his tongue in and out of her ear.

"Umm, babe, what are you doing?" she asked, neglecting the fact she could no longer hide her arousal.

Rayjon placed his hand on her thick thigh and pulled it apart. He trailed his hand down to her center, tracing the lace of her panties, searching for her protruding pussy lips. That is what drove him crazy about her. She had a fat pussy attached to a small frame and it oozed honey almost instantly from his touch.

"I'm trying to hit this box. I know you ain't come all the way from the University of Southern California just for us to have a conversation." He slid his hand into her panties, inserting his middle finger deep into her hot hole.

"Mmmmm," Camryn let out a faint moan, as she arched her back and opened her legs wider, inviting him in. Her tight Prada skirt rose to her waist. "Babe, that shit yo brother did got me freaked out right now. Can we talk about that first and then you fuck me later?" she whined.

Ignoring her request, Rayjon scooped her up into his arms and threw her backward onto the bed. He climbed on top of her and ripped her panties away from her body, throwing them to the floor. "I don't want to tap into your feelings right now. I'm 'bout to kill this pussy."

"But..."

He ripped her tank top down the middle and pushed her knees to her chest, peeling away his boxers in one swift motion.

She then felt his mushroom head slice apart her slippery sex lips.

"Uhh-shit, babe, please take it eas..."

Rayjon slammed his baseball home and felt her pussy suck him in hungrily. He bit into her neck and squeezed her new set of perky twins, before beating her box in.

"Uhh-uhh! Oh shit, baby! Please slow down! Awww shit! Shit!" she moaned loudly, as her first orgasm rattled her body. She felt his thumb twerking her clitoris and his pole stuffing her repeatedly.

"Tell me who Daddy is!" Rayjon demanded, in between strokes. "Tell me who this preppy ass pussy belong to!"

"It's—it's! Ohh shit! It's yours, Rayyy! It's all yours, Daddy! Please fuck me! Fuck me harder!" Camryn cried out in ecstasy, forcing her own knees to her chest, tears visibly rolling down her cheeks. She was obsessed with that thug dick. She damn sure couldn't get it in Bel-air.

She felt him wrap his hand around her neck, slightly choking her, which brought forth her second orgasm.

Once Rayjon felt her release a second time, he flipped her onto her stomach, pulled her toward him and opened her round ass, separating her cheeks. He spit directly on her asshole, took his dick and slid it deep into her backdoor.

Camryn put her hands between her legs and started pinching her clitoris. She loved how Ray fucked her ass. He brought out her inner slut, something no other man had been able to do.

After five minutes of roughly taunting her, Rayjon felt himself reaching his peak. He grabbed a handful of her curls and release his seed deep with her channel. He slowly pulled out and rubbed his piece up and down, in between her ass cheeks.

When their session concluded, they both showered together and returned to the bed. They ate big bowls of Captain Crunch Berries and Rayjon turned on the flat screen, tuning into ESPN, making note of the scores below the screen. He was hoping that LeBron did his thing. He didn't give a fuck about nobody else in the NBA.

"I love you so much, baby," Camryn cooed, scooting closer to him, taking ahold of his dick and planting kisses on his soft head. She was in awe of him. Everything he did caused her to grow more and more obsessed with him. She was damn near hooked. She never imagined any man having that kind of effect on her.

They had met at a Laker's game, while sitting in floor seats. Instead of Rayjon paying attention to the game, or the female on his arm, he spent the entire time trying to come up with her.

She loved his persistence and his looks definitely helped!

Ski Mask Cartel

Two months later, she felt they were going strong, and as much as she was afraid to admit it, she was in love.

"If you love me so much, you'll set up that shit I need, so that I can hit up your sister's husband's bank. I already told you I ain't gon' take more than two hundred G's. I'm tired of bringing this shit up every time, when you already know how I get down."

Camryn swallowed and sat up straight in the bed after placing her bowl of cereal on the night table, next to the lamp. Nervousness took over her and she wanted to regurgitate everything she had just eaten, all over the bed. One thing she hated was disappointing him because that would possibly cause him to kick her to the curb immediately. She didn't know what she'd do if she lost him.

"Baby, just know that I am working on it. As soon as everything falls in line, I'll let you know. I just want to ensure that there won't be any mistakes 'cause I don't want anything happening to you. I'd never be able to live with myself it something went down due to my carelessness." She fidgeted with her fingers, trying to avoid direct eye contact with him.

She didn't know the first thing about robbing a bank and she really didn't want to get involved with it in any way. Her parents were filthy rich.

For as early as she could remember, she'd always been spoiled and given the best of the best. She had a Black card in her purse and she would have let Rayjon spend every penny on it if he wanted to.

In her mind, he didn't have to rob anybody and she had hoped that sooner or later, he'd give up on the urge to do so. She wished that she'd never took him along with her to her sister's wedding. Perhaps, he would have never found out about Stanley's, her sister's husband's, profession.

"I don't need you worrying about me, shorty. I'ma gangsta, and I can hold *me* down. All you gotta do is find out when they have the most money there and a few security codes. I got the rest." He put his bowl on the dresser and popped a stick of gum into his mouth, before sliding into bed next to her, wrapping her into his arms. "Don't you love me, fa real?" he quizzed. He kissed her neck and bit into her jugular vein, licking the length of it.

She shuddered as her nipples grew hard immediately. "Baby, you know that I do, with all of my heart."

He slid his hand between her legs, peeling apart her rose petals. She moaned at the feeling of his two fingers searching for her sweet spot deep within her rosebud.

He sucked on her earlobe. "Listen to me, I'm about my muthafuckin' money and any bitch I fuck wit, gotta be about the same. You hollerin' you tryna be my main bitch, sleepin' all in my mafuckin' bed, got me eatin' yo pussy and shit, but you ain't makin' nothing happen. When you leave my crib today, you better get on bidness or stay yo ass in Bel-air, far away from me. Ain't no use fallin' for you if we ain't got shit in common," Rayjon whispered the last part, two fingers deep inside of her pussy.

Camryn moaned loudly as her eyes rolled to the back of her head. She couldn't afford to lose him. She was already hooked on the street thug and would do *anything* he asked of her.

As his thumb brushed across her pearl, she felt a new orgasm already taking over her. Mentally, she was gone. "Babe—I, uhhh, got you. I'll set things up. I'll do whatever, Daddy. Just please, fuck me 'til I cry." She begged between moans.

Chapter 3

Ajani sat on the hood of his cherry red Audi S6. It was freshly candy painted, sitting on 26-inch Davins, all gold. He'd sent Aiden, his closest cousin, into the corner store to snatch up a box of blunt wraps so they could blow a quarter ounce of Bin Laden.

The sun was shining so bright, that he turned his fitted cap from the back to the front, to shield his eyes. "Man, fuck this! I'm about to snatch up my Ray Bans," he said aloud to himself, jumping off of the hood of the car.

As soon as he did, an all blue drop top '64 Impala pulled up alongside of him, with six niggaz in the car. Before he could open his mouth, five out of the six, pointed assault rifles at him that had clips hanging out of them so long, they looked like they held at least a hundred rounds each.

The passenger next to the driver spoke up. "Say, cuz, you look like you one'a dem Blood niggaz. Am I right?" he asked, mugging Ajani as if his shit stank, ready to knock his head off. The passenger hated all things red and the fact that this nigga was rolling a red Audi meant he was repping that Blood shit extra hard.

Ajani swallowed, curling his upper lip. He looked into the car at each man trying his best to remember each face. "Nigga, fuck Blood. I don't fuck wit them niggaz and they don't fuck wit me. I stand on my own two feet."

One of the niggaz in the backseat who was holding an AK47 with a blue bandana around the handle, sat up. "Yo, cuz, lemme smoke dis brim ass nigga. I know a Blood when I see one." He could already imagine what Ajani would look like with his brains splattered all over the Audi, so he wanted to be the one to do it, remembering how his brother had been slumped by the Bloodz a summer ago.

The fat nigga in the passenger's seat beside the driver, looked back at him and smiled, before focusing back toward

T.J. Edwards

Ajani. "I should let my lil' nigga stank you, homie. You look like one of them Blood niggaz to me."

Ajani couldn't believe they didn't give a fuck about holding him at gun point, while cars drove past. They were literally on a busy street. A city bus had already rolled pass and that didn't stop them from getting ready to splash him. He wished he had a chance to get to the Tech .9 that was under his driver's seat. He had a 50-round clip in there. If he could get to it, he would die trying to kill every nigga in that car, no matter how many bullets he inhaled.

"Say Pee Wee, get out and strip that nigga and snatch up that Audi. We can always paint that mafucka blue later," the fat nigga said, looking toward the backseat.

Pee Wee laid the AR-15 to the side of him and took a .9 millimeter out the small of his back. He jumped out of the car and slammed the barrel into Ajani's chest, as he searched his pockets, uncovering two large bundles of money and an ounce of Bin Laden.

With a snarl on his face, Ajani curled his upper lip, taking mental notes of every nigga that was in the car, including Pee Wee. He swore to himself that if those Crip niggaz allowed him to walk away alive, that he was going to see to it that any mafucka who rocked the color blue would be murdered, until he killed every one of them niggaz that was a part of him being stripped.

He prayed they'd killed him for their sake. He looked across the street and saw Aiden coming out of the store. As soon as he did, they made eye contact and Aiden nodded.

"Damn, cuz, this nigga got about 15 bands on him." Pee Wee snatched the gold rope from around his neck and put the pistol to his neck. "Nigga, open your car door so I can get in. When you do, slide yo bitch ass over and get in the passenger seat," he ordered.

Ajani mugged him with hate. "Nigga, fuck you! Bitch nigga, if you wanna take my shit, you gon' do it on yo own 'cause I ain't helpin' you do shit. What the fuck I look like?"

182

Pee Wee's heart started to beat extremely fast. He was being tested. He was left with no choice. He would have to kill the nigga in broad daylight because there was no way around it. He simply could not let the nigga flex on him like that in front of his crew. That was unacceptable.

Boo-wa! Boo-wa! Boo-wa! Boo-wa!

Ajani saw the driver's head explode, sending blood and brain onto the fat nigga that sat in the passenger seat alongside of him.

Before the studs in the car could make out where the shots were coming from, Aiden was standing over their whip with two .44 Desert Eagles in his hands, finger fucking them like he was in a cowboy movie. Ajani's high yellow cousin had been smart enough to mask up first, but he knew it was him by his build, clothes, and Airmax 90s.

He shot both men in the back seat. They caught face shots and fell forward with their heads resting on the seat in front of them. The fat nigga jumped out of the car and took off running with Aiden bussing at him.

Boo-wa! Boo-wa! Boo-wa!

Ajani took the event and used it as a distraction. As Pee Wee turned around to buss at Aiden, Ajani elbowed him right in the temple, slumping him to his ass. Ajani kneed him in the face, causing his head to bounce off the concrete, knocking him out cold. Reaching under the passenger of his car, he grabbed his nickel-plated .45. He then turned to Pee Wee.

Boom! Boom! Boom!

He delivered three face shots. He nodded at Aiden before jumping into his Audi and smashed out with his left back tire rolling over Pee Wee's leg.

***

"And them bitch niggaz was Crips?" Rayjon asked, slamming a 150-round magazine into the all-black AR .33. He was ready to body some shit. He never took kindly to anybody fucking with his lil' brother. Whenever a nigga did that, he was liable to get his whole family killed including the kids.

Ajani tooted a fat line of cocaine and turned up the bottle of Ace. He felt like the niggaz had caught him slipping. There was no way he was about to take that lying down. He snorted another two lines hard. "Yeah, them niggaz was Crip. The reason they rolled down on me was because of my Audi. Mafucka gon' say I looked like a Blood." He shook his head. "If Aiden wouldn't have come tearin' shit down when he did- mann, them niggaz would have bodied me, ganked me for my stash and took the whip."

Aiden took two strong swallows from the Lean. "Fuck them niggaz, Blood. Yo, at least we knocked all they heads off. I even thought about goin' into the grocery store behind us, and bodyin' everything up in that bitch, just in case they saw some shit, but then I had to think about our mothers. What if some niggaz would have done some shit like that to them?"

Rayjon lowered his head. "Nigga, I don't even wanna think about no shit like that. A mafucka even brush Momma Jersey, I'd try to blow up the whole Los Angeles. That's my heart right there."

"That's why I ain't do it." Aiden said, lighting the blunt of Bin Laden.

He was their first cousin. Momma Jersey and his mother, Rachael, were sisters, and they were extremely close, as were he and his cousins. Aiden and his brother had recently moved over from New Jersey about four months back. His mother wanted a fresh start and to be closer to her sister.

Aiden took a long pull from the blunt. "Bitch niggaz thought it was sweet. They gotta be plugged from over on Normandy 'cuz this whole area is Bloodz and Essays. But the streets talk, so we'll find out exactly where they were plugged from and shut that shit down."

"Yeah." Rayjon agreed, taking the blunt from Aiden. "For now, we gotta fuck over Casper and his lil' crew for my ol' man. Pops say he next on the list to potentially testify against him on that secret indictment he just got word about."

"Wait, what you mean?" Ajani asked, stabbing a small pile of cocaine with his razor blade.

Rayjon blew the thick smoke into the air. "Pop said before they release him in October that they gon' try to come with another indictment. But, as long as we can knock off all of the niggaz that they got lined up to potentially testify against him, they gon' have to drop that shit because they ain't got no legs to stand on. These niggaz would be their only firepower. So, we gotta make mafuckas' hearts acapella. If you know what I mean."

Aiden took the Mach .90 off of his lap and sat it on the table. "No doubt, 'Cuz. Definitely time to make mafuckas stop breathin'. Greed is a good nigga. He ain't ever neglect to make sure my brother and I was straight at all costs. I done seen him give my mother bundles of cash at a time and never asked for shit in return. Yo, kid, ya ol' man got my loyalty. Whatever you niggaz on, I'm just tryna be down with that shit and I'm pretty sure that August is, too," he said, speaking on his little brother.

Ajani looked over to Rayjon who was rubbing his chin. He loved both of his cousins. He knew when it came down to making them guns bark, that both men were young killers with no heart.

Having Aiden and August on the team would up the ante. Not only could they knock off his father's enemy list, but they could also get their weight all the way up, by hitting a bunch of licks along the way. And since they had grown up together, and related by blood, there was a definite trust factor there. He started to imagine the possibilities.

"Nigga, if you get down with us, we gon' definitely put some bands in your pocket. We got a list of our own that's about to put us on the road to riches. I'm talking crazy commas. But, shit get real bloody because you can't have no mercy. We executin' bitchez and all."

Aiden shrugged his shoulders. "How much cake we talkin' about?" As long as the numbers were right, he didn't give a fuck about whose head they knocked off. Killing a female didn't mean nothing to him because a female could kill you just as fast as a man could.

Their Aunt Princess was the perfect example of that. Her and her husband, Taurus, were savages. Relentless killers and Princess's body count was stacked higher than his. So, in his mind, a bitch could get it, too.

"Give us a few months and you should see real close to a mill. That's not including narcotics," Rayjon reassured him, slipping the bulletproof vest over his head.

Ajani nodded in agreeance, securing his bulletproof vest into place, as well. "Nigga, we finna eat. Let's turn up!"

"Word is bond, shit finna get real bloody."

Available Now!

Ski Mask Cartel
<u>Coming Soon from Lock Down Publications/Ca$h Presents</u>

BOW DOWN TO MY GANGSTA

By **Ca$h**

TORN BETWEEN TWO

By **Coffee**

BLOOD STAINS OF A SHOTTA **II**

By **Jamaica**

WHEN THE STREETS CLAP BACK **II**

By **Jibril Williams**

STEADY MOBBIN

By **Marcellus Allen**

BLOOD OF A BOSS **V**

By **Askari**

BRIDE OF A HUSTLA **III**

By **Destiny Skai**

WHEN A GOOD GIRL GOES BAD **II**

By **Adrienne**

LOVE & CHASIN' PAPER **II**

By **Qay Crockett**

THE HEART OF A GANGSTA **III**

By **Jerry Jackson**

LOYAL TO THE GAME **IV**

By **T.J. & Jelissa**

A DOPEBOY'S PRAYER **II**

By **Eddie "Wolf" Lee**

IF LOVING YOU IS WRONG... **III**

By **Jelissa**

T.J. Edwards

BLOODY COMMAS **III**

SKI MASK CARTEL

By **T.J. Edwards**

BLAST FOR ME **II**

By **Ghost**

A DISTINGUISHED THUG STOLE MY HEART **III**

By **Meesha**

ADDICTIED TO THE DRAMA **II**

By **Jamila Mathis**

LIPSTICK KILLAH II

By **Mimi**

Available Now

RESTRAINING ORDER **I & II**

By **CA$H & Coffee**

LOVE KNOWS NO BOUNDARIES **I II & III**

By **Coffee**

RAISED AS A GOON I, II & III

By **Ghost**

LAY IT DOWN **I & II**

LAST OF A DYING BREED

By **Jamaica**

LOYAL TO THE GAME

LOYAL TO THE GAME II

LOYAL TO THE GAME III

By **TJ & Jelissa**

BLOODY COMMAS I & II

By **T.J. Edwards**

Ski Mask Cartel

IF LOVING HIM IS WRONG...I & II

By **Jelissa**

WHEN THE STREETS CLAP BACK

By **Jibril Williams**

A DISTINGUISHED THUG STOLE MY HEART I & II

By **Meesha**

PUSH IT TO THE LIMIT

By **Bre' Hayes**

BLOOD OF A BOSS **I, II, III & IV**

By **Askari**

THE STREETS BLEED MURDER **I, II & III**

THE HEART OF A GANGSTA I & II

By **Jerry Jackson**

CUM FOR ME

CUM FOR ME 2

CUM FOR ME 3

An **LDP Erotica Collaboration**

BRIDE OF A HUSTLA **I & II**

THE FETTI GIRLS **I, II& III**

By **Destiny Skai**

WHEN A GOOD GIRL GOES BAD

By **Adrienne**

A GANGSTER'S REVENGE **I II III & IV**

THE BOSS MAN'S DAUGHTERS

THE BOSS MAN'S DAUGHTERS II

A SAVAGE LOVE **I & II**

BAE BELONGS TO ME

A HUSTLER'S DECEIT I, II

T.J. Edwards

By **Aryanna**

A KINGPIN'S AMBITON

A KINGPIN'S AMBITION **II**

I MURDER FOR THE DOUGH

By **Ambitious**

TRUE SAVAGE

TRUE SAVAGE II

TRUE SAVAGE **III**

By **Chris Green**

A DOPEBOY'S PRAYER

By **Eddie "Wolf" Lee**

WHAT ABOUT US **I & II**

NEVER LOVE AGAIN

THUG ADDICTION

By **Kim Kaye**

THE KING CARTEL **I, II & III**

By **Frank Gresham**

THESE NIGGAS AIN'T LOYAL **I, II & III**

By **Nikki Tee**

GANGSTA SHYT **I II &III**

By **CATO**

THE ULTIMATE BETRAYAL

By **Phoenix**

BOSS'N UP **I , II & III**

By **Royal Nicole**

I LOVE YOU TO DEATH

By **Destiny J**

I RIDE FOR MY HITTA

Ski Mask Cartel

T.J. Edwards

BOOKS BY LDP'S CEO, CA$H

TRUST IN NO MAN

TRUST IN NO MAN 2

TRUST IN NO MAN 3

BONDED BY BLOOD

SHORTY GOT A THUG

THUGS CRY

THUGS CRY 2

THUGS CRY 3

TRUST NO BITCH

TRUST NO BITCH 2

TRUST NO BITCH 3

TIL MY CASKET DROPS

RESTRAINING ORDER

RESTRAINING ORDER 2

IN LOVE WITH A CONVICT

Coming Soon

BONDED BY BLOOD 2

BOW DOWN TO MY GANGSTA